**"You shouldn't have lied to your grandmother,"
Rhys said.**

Startled, Lani looked at him. "When did I lie to
her?"

"When you told her I wasn't interested in you.
Did you tell her that so she would call off her
watchdogs, or because you really believe it?"

She picked up a handful of sand and let it run
through her fingers.

"Both."

His hand closed around hers. "I guess I'll have
to change your mind."

A current of heat radiated up her arm. Awareness
simmered through her, and all he had done was
take her hand. She didn't want to think of what
would happen to her if he touched her more
intimately. Yet she wanted nothing more.

"I've gone past being interested to being strongly
attracted," Rhys said. "No matter who tries to
stand between us, it won't make any difference."

"Make any difference about what?"

"About making love to you. I've thought of
nothing else since we met."

She tried to ignore the heat flooding through
her at his words. "You can think about it all you
want, but it doesn't mean it's going to happen."

He lifted her hand to his mouth, brushing his
lips over her skin. "Oh, it's going to happen. It's
just a matter of when." Her breath caught as he
gently sucked on first one finger, then another.
When his teeth nipped her soft flesh, desire raced
through her. She was unaware of the expression of
longing in her eyes as his lips tantalized her flesh.

But Rhys saw her green eyes darken with passion,
and triumph filled him. She wanted him as much
as he wanted her. . . .

WHAT ARE *LOVESWEPT* ROMANCES?

They are stories of true romance and touching emotion. We believe those two very important ingredients are constants in our highly sensual and very believable stories in the *LOVESWEPT* line. Our goal is to give you, the reader, stories of consistently high quality that may sometimes make you laugh, sometimes make you cry, but are always fresh and creative and contain many delightful surprises within their pages.

Most romance fans read an enormous number of books. Those they truly love, they keep. Others may be traded with friends and soon forgotten. We hope that each *LOVESWEPT* romance will be a treasure—a "keeper." We will always try to publish

LOVE STORIES YOU'LL NEVER FORGET
BY AUTHORS YOU'LL ALWAYS REMEMBER

The Editors

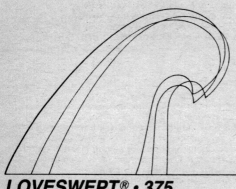

LOVESWEPT® • 375

Patt Bucheister
Once Burned,
Twice As Hot

 BANTAM BOOKS
NEW YORK • TORONTO • LONDON • SYDNEY • AUCKLAND

ONCE BURNED, TWICE AS HOT

A Bantam Book / January 1990

*If you would be interested in receiving protective vinyl
covers for your Loveswept books, please write to this address
for information:*

Loveswept
Bantam Books
P.O. Box 985
Hicksville, NY 11802

ISBN 0-553-44016-0

Published simultaneously in the United States and Canada

PRINTED IN THE UNITED STATES OF AMERICA

O   0 9 8 7 6 5 4 3 2 1

One

One knee was skinned and the palms of her hands were scraped and stinging, but they were the only injuries Lani Makena sustained when she was knocked down.

One moment she was running by the four-mile marker, waving to a friend in the half-marathon race. The next thing Lani knew, she was down on her hands and one knee in the middle of the street. She had expected to have a few discomforts running the thirteen-mile race, but she hadn't thought she was going to slam into a padded brick wall. At least that's what it had felt like.

From somewhere above her, she heard a cross male voice exclaim, "Bloody hell!"

What made her look up to see the man's face instead of checking her injuries wasn't what he said as much as the way he had said it. It was the first time anyone had ever sworn at her in a clipped British accent.

He towered over her, a man in his early thirties. Unsmiling as he stared down at her, he stood with his feet slightly apart, his stance one of power and authority. Dressed in a three-piece dark wool suit, white shirt, and gray silk tie, he obviously wasn't a participant in the race. His eyes were grayish blue, the color of the sea during a storm. She thought she detected pain in the depths of those eyes, and put it down to the sun's glare. His sandy blond hair was being gently tousled by the wind, and Lani decided he was the most strikingly handsome man she had ever seen. It was a shame he wasn't smiling.

Ignoring the other runners passing by, he knelt down on one knee and asked, "Are you all right?"

She attempted to get up, putting the palm of her hand onto the road for balance, then grimaced as her tender skin came in contact with the hot pavement.

"I've been better."

Rhys's fingers curled around her arm, and as he stood up he hoisted her to her feet. Drawing her to the side of the road, he slid his hands down her arms to examine her palms. Her skin was scraped and bleeding slightly. Grains of sand were embedded in her flesh. He took a handkerchief out of his pocket and dabbed at the torn skin to remove some of the grit.

"Ouch." She tried to tug her hand out of his. "What are you trying to do, finish what the road started?"

"This wouldn't have happened," he said, "if you had been watching where you were going."

Despite the bite in his voice, his touch was lighter, gentler, and oddly soothing. She glanced up. "Or if *you* hadn't been in my way."

Puzzled by the odd sensation of warmth running up her arm, she studied him carefully. The rays of the late-morning Hawaiian sun beat down on them, making his choice of clothing definitely unsuitable. His attire would have been appropriate in most other parts of the United States in February, but in Hawaii, the temperature was over eighty degrees. Evidently he had just arrived and hadn't had a chance to change clothes. He had to be uncomfortable. She decided that was probably why he was so cranky. But that didn't explain why he had been in the road during a race.

Smiling faintly, she said, "You're going to be in worse shape than me if you stay in those clothes much longer."

Rhys Jones looked up from her scraped palms and found himself staring at her mouth. Then he raised his gaze to her glittering, almond-shaped green eyes. Like the other marathon contestants he had seen, she wore running shorts and a tank top. A sheet of thin white plastic with a black number printed on it was pinned to the front of the shirt. Her shorts were white, emphasizing her tanned legs, and her sky blue top was of a clinging knit fabric. Her strawberry blond hair was pulled back in a thick ponytail, several softly waving tendrils brushing her cheeks. His gaze returned to her mouth as he wondered why her wry smile was so captivating. Then it dawned on him that he was still holding her hands.

He must be more tired than he thought.

His gaze dropped to the number fourteen pinned to her shirt. "Is that your age?"

She made a scolding sound. "Someone got up on the wrong side of the bed this morning," she said, but kindly.

"The problem is there was no bed."

Without explaining his remark, he wrapped his handkerchief around her palm and dropped her hand. Hiking up his slacks, he bent so he could examine the abrasions on her leg. She'd landed on one knee, and the damage was more severe than on her hands. With a light touch, he brushed off particles of sand.

Lani didn't move away, even though each stroke was painful. When his fingers inadvertently slipped behind her knee as his thumb flicked away a small piece of gravel, she felt something other than pain. A feathery sensation of warmth flowed along her thigh, and it had nothing to do with the heat from the sun.

When he straightened, he looked down at her. "Maybe you should have a doctor check your injury."

She shook her head. "I don't need to see a doctor. They're only scratches." She glanced at several other runners as they passed by. "I need to get back in the race before I cool off too much."

"Under the circumstances, that would be incredibly stupid, don't you think?"

She didn't take offense. "Probably, but entering this race wasn't exactly a stroke of genius to start with. I keep telling myself it's all for a good cause since it's for charity." She let her gaze slowly trail over him from his polished leather shoes to his silk tie. "Speaking of stupid, what were you doing in the middle of the street during a race?"

"I was trying to cross it when you ran into me."

She frowned. "You make it sound as though this was all my fault." She tapped the number pinned on her top. "I'm the one who is supposed to be in the street, not you."

"Look, lady. I haven't had any sleep in what seems like a month. I'm tired, I'm hot, and I'm not in the mood to argue with you. I've gone through more time zones than I care to count. All I want to do right now is check in to my hotel, take a nice long shower, and sleep for two days. I'm sorry you've been hurt. It wasn't intentional."

"You don't have any luggage," she said.

Exasperation tightened his jaw. "The taxi driver let me out where the street was blocked off." He gestured toward the Outrigger Hotel they were standing in front of. "The driver is going to deliver my luggage to the hotel when he can. Does that ease your mind?"

Lani fought back the urge to smile at the dry sarcasm in his voice. He probably wouldn't appreciate the fact that she was amused.

"Yes. Thank you," she replied with mock seriousness.

"I'm relieved," he said with equal mockery in his tone.

Gesturing toward the wooden barriers at the intersection, she asked, "Don't they have barricades where you come from?"

He glanced at the barriers, then brought his gaze back to her. "Yes," he murmured cautiously. "Why?"

"Do you ignore them there, too?"

A corner of his mouth twitched. "I can't remember feeling the need before today."

One of the other runners called out to her as he jogged past. "Hey, Lani. Run out of gas already?"

She laughed. "I'll have a hard time living this down."

The sound of her laughter was rich, and as intoxicating as warm honey in whiskey. "Is that your name? Lani?"

"My name is Kapiolani Makena. Lani for short."

His gaze went to her reddish blond hair and green eyes. Surprise overcame his normal tact. "You're Hawaiian?"

"My mother was half-Hawaiian." She wasn't about to go into her ancestry with this stranger. It was none of his business and not her favorite subject. "Well," she said with resignation, "I have a race to run."

Rhys was oddly reluctant to see her go. "I can't persuade you to rest rather than run?"

She shook her head. "Not a chance." Tilting her head to one side, she added with amusement, "It's been nice running into you. I hope you enjoy your stay on the island. Aloha."

As Lani began to lengthen her stride away from the overdressed stranger, she wondered why she felt both relief and disappointment at leaving him. The contradiction was as puzzling as her reaction when he had held her hand and touched the soft skin behind her knee. It didn't matter, she told herself. She wouldn't be seeing him again. She should be concentrating on the nine more miles she had to run instead of thinking about one of the tourists.

Either stubbornness or pride kept her running, even though each time she bent her leg, her knee caused her discomfort. She wasn't going to give her cousin Kimo the satisfaction of saying he was right. The previous year he had teased her unmercifully about not finishing the race, and she was determined to complete this one if she had to crawl over the finish line. Which might be the only way she would make it. There were at least a hundred different ways she would have preferred to spend a Saturday than plodding along mile after mile.

Her fingers curled around the soft cloth still wrapped around her hand. She had forgotten she had the stranger's handkerchief. Ahead of her was a trash can placed alongside the road, but she passed it without tossing the soiled cloth inside.

An hour and a half later Lani saw the banner stretched high over the street announcing the end of the race. Grinning, she thought *finish line* had to be the two most beautiful words in the

English language. Now all she had to do was force her legs to keep moving so she could make it under the banner.

She was drenched in perspiration, and every muscle in her body was protesting. A number of participants had completed the race before her, but she didn't mind. When she had entered the half-marathon, she hadn't expected to win, hadn't even wanted to. Her goal had been to finish.

With a feeling of exhilaration, she ran under the banner. The crowd waiting at the finish line applauded her and the others who crossed with her. Walking stiffly, she moved away from the crowd, then stopped. Her hands on her knees, she bent over to catch her breath.

Her cousin Kimo, who had also run, made his way through the throngs of people watching the finish. Kimo was a hundred pounds heavier than Lani, a tall and well-built Hawaiian with dark eyes and long thick black hair. He had removed his shirt and shoes after finishing the race, not bothered by the hot pavement on the soles of his bare feet. A towel was draped around his thick neck, and he held a large paper cup in his hand as he approached Lani.

He emptied the cup over her head.

From some distance away, Rhys watched as Lani lifted her face to the water cascading over her head. He could hear her laughter when she was picked up by the large man and whirled around. Then she was set back on her feet and the man handed her the towel from around his neck. Before drying off, she tore off the band holding her hair and shook her head to loosen the dampened waves.

Rhys stayed where he was, watching the woman. He felt foolish for following the impulse to see her again, and it wasn't a feeling he liked much. Earlier, in his hotel room, he had taken a shower and changed into cooler clothing, irritated when he continued to think about the woman with strawberry blond hair.

The dull ache at the base of his neck warned him that he should be taking his doctor's advice and resting. Years of working long hours seven days a week had caught up with him, causing blinding migraines. This was supposed to be a much-needed holiday. After he took care of that little business his partner had tacked on at the last minute.

He had been asked to find another woman, not to chase after the green-eyed one he had met briefly in the middle of a road.

So why had he asked the desk clerk where the end of the race was? he wondered. It didn't make any more sense than leaving his room instead of catching up on his sleep. When he had arrived at the finish line, he'd watched every woman running under the banner, looking for one particular runner. It was ridiculous, he had chided himself. She wasn't the type of woman he was usually attracted to. He had always preferred women who were more tailored, neat and tidy in appearance and habits. The little he had seen of Lani Makena, she was none of those things. Yet there was something about her that had drawn him to the finish line to wait for her.

Now he watched her every movement as she used the towel on her legs, surprised when a flash of heat seared through him as she stroked her inner thigh. She grimaced when she touched her injured knee, and he started toward her.

The tall dark-haired man was talking to her as Rhys approached. "I haven't seen you with skinned knees since you were five, Maia."

She hooked the towel around her neck. "I had a run-in with the road, and the road won."

Expecting a teasing comment, Lani glanced up when Kimo didn't say anything. Her cousin's gaze had shifted from her to somewhere over her shoulder. Turning her head, she saw the man who had been the cause of her injuries standing behind her.

He looked cooler and much more comfortable in a dark tan shirt and white slacks. Whatever work he did, he did it well and was paid generously, she thought as she recognized designer labels on his shirt and leather belt.

She was surprised that she was pleased to see him, and wondered why he was there. It could be a coincidence or intentional. Since he wore dark glasses, it was impossible to read any expression in his eyes. Maybe it was just as well, she decided. Some things were better not known.

He held a large paper cup out to her. "I don't suggest you pour this over your head. It will do you more good if you drink it."

Her fingers wrapped around the cup, brushing against his briefly. "Thanks," she murmured.

He waited until she had taken a generous drink of the fruit juice. "You don't seem surprised to see me."

She shrugged. "I don't surprise easily."

"Apparently not. I thought you said your name is Lani."

"It is."

"Then why did he call you Maia?"

She took another sip of the drink, closing her eyes for a moment as she relished the cool refreshing taste in her dry throat. "This is wonderful." Opening her eyes, she answered his question. "He calls me Maia because I once had a yellow bathing suit I loved. I wore it all the time."

"What does a yellow bathing suit have to do with him calling you Maia?"

"Maia means banana. Apparently that's what I resembled when I was six."

"It's amazing what a few years will do for a girl," Rhys drawled, a hint of a smile around his mouth.

Kimo placed his large hands on his hips and scowled. "Maia, you know this guy?"

Lani recognized the stony glint in Kimo's eyes. She was accustomed to the protectiveness of the male members of her family, but she couldn't expect a stranger to understand it or want to put up with it.

In an attempt to defuse what could turn into an unpleasant few minutes, she started to introduce the two men. Gesturing with the hand holding the cup, she said, "This is my cousin, Kimo Makena. I'm sorry, but I don't know your name."

"Rhys Jones," he supplied, pronouncing his Christian name as Reece.

She continued with the introductions. "Kimo, this is Rhys Jones. Be nice to him. He's had a rough day."

The two men shook hands, each assessing the other carefully. Dropping his hand, Kimo asked bluntly, "Are you here on business or pleasure, Mr. Jones?"

"Business."

"Will it take long?"

"I hope not."

Apparently, Kimo had gotten the answers he wanted. He brought his attention back to Lani. "I'll see you later at Tutu's party."

Lani nodded. "I'll be there. Bianca and I are using Sally's apartment to shower and change before we go."

Kimo gave Rhys one last long look before walking away, but Rhys didn't notice. He was gazing at Lani. Her hair was drying quickly, but her wet knit shirt clung to her rib cage and breasts like a second skin. The number pinned to her top barely kept her decent.

He brought his gaze up to her green eyes and couldn't look away. "Are you up to going to a party after running twenty-six miles?"

She returned the cup to him. "Actually the race was only thirteen miles. It's a half-marathon." She smiled faintly. "Is that your polite way of saying I look like hell?"

He wanted to touch her. The realization stunned him. He settled for taking a corner of the towel and catching a drop of moisture on her jawline. Something in her eyes changed when he let the towel trail down her neck. He wasn't too exhausted not to recognize the signs of attraction when he saw them.

"Your knee and hands are scraped," he said, "and you've been running steadily for several hours. I wouldn't think you'd be in a party mood."

"Whether I feel like it or not, I have to go. It's my grandmother's birthday. Death is the only excuse for not being there."

Lani heard her name being called and looked around. One of the other runners was limping toward her. The woman's long black hair was tied back and hung down to her waist. Like Lani, she wore a number on her shirt. Unlike Lani, she was frowning.

She was still breathing heavily as she stopped in front of them. "I don't know why I let you talk me into this, Lani. I have two blisters on my right foot and a cramp in my leg." Amusement filled her dark eyes when she glanced down and saw the condition of Lani's leg. "Now I don't feel so bad. Did you crawl the last mile or two?"

Lani laughed. "No. I had a slight accident."

"It was my fault," Rhys said.

Bianca looked from Lani to the man at her side. "Really? What did you do?"

"I knocked her down."

Bianca pursed her lips and a whistled softly under her breath. "Lani, you have all the luck. I get blisters, and you bump into a gorgeous man." Her voice held a wealth of mocking self-pity. "Life is not fair."

Rhys smiled. "I don't think Lani enjoyed the experience."

"Lani's that way." She held out her hand. "I'm her cousin, Bianca Loa."

He clasped her hand briefly. "Rhys Jones. You're the second cousin of Lani's I've met in the last ten minutes. How many more are there?"

Bianca blinked. "I don't know. I've never counted all of them." She turned to Lani. "Who did he meet?"

"Kimo."

Bianca whistled again. "And he's still standing?"

Lani saw the puzzled look on Rhys's face and explained. "Kimo tends to be a little protective because he considers us twins." She laughed lightly at his stunned expression. "We were born on the same day. Different parents."

"Saying Kimo is a little protective," Bianca said dryly, "is like saying a shark is an itty-bitty fish. I'm glad Kimo's left you in one piece to enjoy your visit to our island, Mr. Jones. How long are you going to stay?"

Rhys lifted a brow at her blunt question. "Only long enough to take care of some business. Then I'm going on to Australia."

Like Kimo, Bianca seemed satisfied with his answer and turned to Lani. "We need to get going. We have to change before we leave for Makaha."

Rhys's gaze narrowed as he looked down at Lani. "Makaha? Is that where you live?"

Puzzled by the change in his tone of voice, she answered, "It's where my grandmother lives. Why?"

"The business I have to take care of while I'm in Hawaii deals with a woman who lives in Makaha. Perhaps you know her."

When Lani didn't say anything, Bianca asked, "What's her name."

"Anne McGregor."

Both women stared at him, astonishment widening their eyes. Then they slowly turned their heads and looked at each other.

"Obviously you know her," he drawled.

"Why do you want to see Anne McGregor?" Lani asked.

"As I said, it's business," he said flatly, making it clear that what he meant was it was none of *her* business. "Perhaps you can tell me how I can find her."

Biting her bottom lip, Lani hesitated. Then she said, "I won't do that unless you tell me why you want her."

Irritation tightened his jaw. "For fear of being rude, I can only say my business is with Anne McGregor, not you."

Bianca made a choking sound, and Lani gave her a quelling look. What was going on? Rhys wondered. Both women clearly knew Anne McGregor, and it was just as obvious neither of them wanted to talk about her. To find that Lani knew the woman he had come to see was an unbelievable coincidence. And he was going to take advantage of it.

Reaching into his back pocket, he withdrew his wallet. He took a business card from it and handed it to her. Over Lani's shoulder, her cousin read out loud, " 'Rhys Berkeley-Jones, solicitor, Smythe, Pritchard and Jones, London, England.' " Raising her gaze, she asked, "Solicitor? Does that mean you're a salesman, Mr. Jones?"

"It means I'm a lawyer, Miss Loa."

Bianca grinned. "Do you wear one of those funny curled white wigs and a black robe that we see in the movies?"

"I'm in international law. I'm usually in boardrooms, not courtrooms." He also corrected the pronunciation of his name, stating it was Reece, not Rice, and Barkeley, not Berkeley.

Lani returned his card to him. "There seems to be a great deal about you that isn't as it appears, including your name. Why did you tell me your name was Rhys Jones?"

"Because it is. I don't use the hyphenated part of my name. It sounds too pretentious and that's something I'm not. It's important that I find Miss McGregor. I have some legal matters to discuss with her on behalf of a client in England."

Again, he saw the two women exchange glances. For some reason, they didn't like the fact that he wanted to see Anne McGregor. "I would appreciate any assistance you could give me in finding her."

Lani made a decision. "Anne will be at the luau my family is having for my grandmother's birthday later today. If you would like to come with us, perhaps you could talk to her there."

"Are you crazy!" Bianca exclaimed softly.

"I know what I'm doing," Lani said under her breath. Keeping her gaze on Rhys, she asked, "Well, Mr. Jones? Would you like to go to the luau with us?"

He noticed Lani didn't sound particularly enthusiastic about him going with her, which made him wonder why she was inviting him at all. He was going to find out.

"It would save me a lot of time," he said, "if I can see Anne McGregor tonight. This job was thrown at me at the last moment, and I would like to get it out of the way as soon as possible."

Lani nodded. "I can promise you she'll be there. You'll have to wait for us to change our clothes at a friend's apartment. Then we'll go to Makaha."

An hour later Rhys sat beside Lani in her car with Bianca in the back as they drove away from Waikiki. Both women had showered and changed into colorful Hawaiian pareaus, long saronglike dresses. Instead of running shoes they wore comfortable sandals.

Rhys was still recovering from his shock at seeing Lani as she came out of her friend's bedroom. His mouth had gone dry and his heart had thudded uncomfortably. The colorful strapless gown clung to her breasts and hips and tapered down to her ankles. There was a slit up one side, giving him a tantalizing glimpse of a tanned leg when she walked. The flowers on the dark blue material were the same color as her reddish blond hair, but he scarcely noticed that. It was the woman that held his attention.

As they drove along he gave the cane fields a cursory glance when Bianca pointed them out to him, his attention returning immediately to Lani. The palm trees and views of the ocean were given the same brief acknowledgment. He preferred to look at her. Her hair was longer than he'd originally thought, falling in waves down her back. Occasionally, the breeze coming through the open window lifted the ends of her hair gently. The slit in her dress was gaping open, leaving a tempting view of her thigh as she drove.

Bianca chattered most of the way to Makaha, telling Rhys about some of the sights he should see on the island. Lani concentrated on her driving, although she knew the way by heart. She had invited the Englishman on impulse, figuring it was better to know where he was and what he was doing as he searched for Anne McGregor.

When they were in the privacy of their friend's bedroom, Bianca had again told Lani she was crazy. Lani was beginning to think her cousin was right. Rhys Jones didn't impress her as the type of man who appreciated someone playing games with him.

She had another reason for asking Rhys to go to the luau, though, which she hadn't mentioned to Bianca. She was puzzled by her reaction to him. Coming from a demonstrative family, she was accustomed to physical contact with people. But his touch was different. *He* was different, she clarified, and it wasn't just his accent or his appearance. It was her response to him that was so unlike anything she had ever experienced before. She felt a strange electricity along her nerve endings when he was near, an awareness she couldn't define with any one word.

She wasn't even sure she liked what she was feeling. Or maybe she liked it too much.

Her grandmother's house was a large sprawling wooden structure built over seventy years ago on a peninsula of land jutting out into the ocean. The sound of music and people laughing and talking could be heard as they walked around the side of the house to where the luau was being held. Tiny lights were strung in the trees and across the lanai, a concrete patio extending from the rear of the house. Tiki torches were positioned at various intervals across the grounds, adding a festive touch. Waves crashed on the shore in the background. Music was provided by four men with guitars and two on drums.

After one last serious glance at Lani, Bianca left them as they walked through the back gate. Rhys caught the look and again wondered why Bianca appeared to be warning Lani about something.

Lani led Rhys across the yard, introducing him to members of her family, telling everyone why he was there. Each time she mentioned he had traveled to Hawaii for the sole purpose of finding Anne McGregor, he was subjected to looks that ranged from wary to curious to shocked. He met aunts, uncles, cousins, nieces, and nephews, and friends with names like Kale, Pilipo, Mei, Loke, and Kaniela. There were also common names he was more familiar with, but it would have been impossible for him to remember all the names, even if he hadn't been suffering from jet lag.

He was made to feel welcome in a guarded fashion. There was nothing definite he could pin down about their attitude other than receiving cautious looks and feeling that every move he made was being watched.

He caught one person in particular staring at him whenever he happened to look in her direction, her dark eyes drilling into him with a curious intensity. She was also the one person Lani neglected to include in the introductions. When he asked who the woman was, Lani told him she was her grandmother, Emma Makena. The older woman made an impressive picture as she sat in a rattan peacock chair like a queen with her subjects around her. She was a plump woman dressed in an enveloping black muumuu with puffy sleeves. Threads of gray were woven through the thick black hair piled on top of her stately head. A large red hibiscus blossom was over one ear, and around her neck she wore a lei of slender green leaves and another of white and yellow plumeria blossoms.

Lani guided him over to one of the buffet tables, which was laden with all sorts of food. He hadn't the faintest idea what most of the various concoctions were. When he asked, Lani furnished him with the names, but they were mostly Hawaiian and didn't help him much. She filled a plate with lomi salmon, fried rice, luau pork, fresh pineapple, and shrimp tempura and handed it to him. One of the women behind the table offered him a wine cooler, a slice of lemon floating on the top. Alcoholic beverages were one of the items on the list of don'ts from his doctor, so he accepted it but didn't drink it. Besides, the last thing he should be doing was drinking something that had a kick like a hot-tempered mule when he was so exhausted. Each step he took felt like he was walking in taffy anyway. A couple of sips of the potent wine would have him falling on his face.

Plate in one hand and glass in the other, he turned to Lani. She wasn't there. Instead, Kimo stood beside him. It was not a change he welcomed. The large man offered him a place to sit at one of the tables scattered around the yard. Kimo sat down across from him and a few other male members of Lani's family joined them. Rhys couldn't decide if he was becoming paranoid or if they were all actually guarding him.

What had started out as a fairly straightforward business excursion was becoming oddly complicated. As far as he knew, Anne McGregor had nothing to hide, so it didn't make sense that everyone was shielding her from him. Unfortunately, as tired as he was, nothing much made sense. Like the way he was attracted to Lani Makena.

While he stabbed his fork into the various bits of food on his plate, he listened to Kimo repeat basically word for word the travelog Bianca had recited during the drive to the luau. He made the appropriate comments with as much grace as he could muster, deciding he would go along with being manipulated for the time being. They could play their little games all night, as long as he eventually got to meet the blasted woman his partner had insisted he see.

While Kimo continued his discourse on the flora and fauna of Hawaii, Rhys let his gaze wander. The sun was beginning to sink below the horizon, creating a breathtaking sunset. Rhys removed his dark glasses and stuck them in his breast pocket. Glancing over toward Lani's grandmother, he was surprised to see Lani kneeling down by the older woman's chair. Even from a distance, he could tell she was talking seriously to her grandmother, and whatever she was saying was not something her grandmother wanted to hear. As he watched, Lani's grandmother shook her head vehemently, and her sharp gaze was hostile when she looked up to stare directly at him.

Lani slowly straightened, standing motionless for a moment before bending over to kiss her grandmother's cheek. Then she raised her head and looked at him, too, her expression oddly sad. She smiled faintly and turned away to go into the house.

Rhys frowned. There were more undercurrents here than in the ocean.

He didn't see any signal or hear any announcement, but all of a sudden everyone began moving to sit or stand in a half circle in front of Emma. Kimo nudged Rhys's arm and jerked his head, which apparently was an invitation for him to join the others. He stood in the back, waiting with everyone else. But they knew what they were waiting for. He didn't.

Standing to one side of the older woman's chair, a white-haired man lifted a large conch shell to his mouth and blew several long, rather mournful notes. Drums began to beat. The sliding-glass doors behind Lani's grandmother opened and women in two lines stepped out in unison to the music of the guitars and drums. Lani was the third in line on the left. They formed two rows in front of Emma, all of them wearing identical leis of white and yellow plumerias.

Rhys had seen samples of the hula in movies and on television, but here there were no commercially manufactured green plastic skirts or steel guitars. He saw the beauty and grace of the entire dance as it was meant to be done. The Hawaiian words the women sang were accompanied by graceful movements as beautiful and as sensual as the drumbeats. Each motion of their hands told the story that particular dance communicated.

For a moment he took in the whole picture—the swaying hips, the fluid gestures of the hands and arms, the rhythmic movement of bare feet on green grass. But as his gaze roamed down the line of dancing figures the sight of Lani caught and held his attention. He was only able to see her in brief glimpses since she was in the front line and those behind her occasionally blocked his view. What he could see was enough to make him want to see more. Kimo followed him as he walked around behind the others to one side where fewer people were standing.

Rhys didn't hear the drums or guitars. He didn't see any of the other dancers. Lani's enchanting movements fired his imagination and held him enthralled. He had never considered the hula an erotic form of dance . . . until now. The flowing swing of her hips made him want to feel her move against him in the exact same way. As she stepped two paces to the left, then two to the right, the slit in her dress teased him with glimpses of her thigh. The primal sensuality of each motion and gesture awakened in him a primitive response as old as time. Desire writhed through him, more urgent and stronger than he had ever felt.

He wondered how long this dance was going to last. It was driving him crazy watching Lani. *She* was driving him crazy. Or maybe he was crazy already. The doctor had said he was going to be in deep trouble if he didn't take some time off. Evidently, the learned physician was right.

When the music ended, the women glided off the grass to stand behind Emma as another woman began to sing in Hawaiian. Five little girls dressed in halter tops and skirts made of ti leaves stepped out of the house alongside small boys dressed in white shirts and pants, red sashes around their waists. They did a charming variety of movements, their expressions mostly serious. Rhys smiled when he saw one of the boys' lips moving, as if he were counting each step.

When the dancing was through, it was time to get down to some serious eating. Children raced to the buffet tables, followed more slowly by the adults. A plate was filled with food and carried to the woman in the peacock chair.

Rhys waited for Lani to come to him. When she didn't, he went to her. His patience, as well as his stamina, was running out. He needed to go back to his hotel and get some sleep or he was going to be a zombie. A zombie with a killer headache. But first he wanted to get the Anne McGregor business out of the way. Since Lani knew the woman and coming to the luau had been Lani's idea, she was going to tell him where the woman was.

Kimo remained glued to his side as he walked across the grass to where Lani was talking to several other women. He was becoming irritated with the bulky Hawaiian shadowing him. In fact, he was becoming annoyed with a number of things.

Lani happened to look up and saw Rhys walking toward her, determination in the set of his jaw and his long stride. With the help of her family, she had managed to stall the meeting of the Englishman and Anne McGregor. Seeing the look of impatience on his face, she had the feeling she had run out of time. He was going to insist on meeting Anne McGregor, and she couldn't think of any valid reason not to introduce them.

"It's all right, Kimo," she said quietly when it looked as though her cousin was ready to step between them. "You go get something to eat."

The other women faded away with Kimo, leaving her alone with Rhys. She took a deep steadying breath, then asked politely, "Have you been enjoying the luau, Mr. Jones?"

"It's been a unique experience. So is having a bodyguard. I can't remember having anyone think I needed one before."

Strong wind off the ocean was blowing her hair, and she lifted a hand to hold it back from her face. "You have a vivid imagination, Mr. Jones. You could have left anytime you wanted."

"I had a purpose in coming here, and you know what it is."

She sighed heavily. "You want to meet Anne McGregor."

"Either tonight or tomorrow or even the next day. I will find her, with or without your help. I don't know why you and your family are attempting to protect her or hide her or whatever in hell you're doing. I've come to give her something, not to harm her or hurt her in any way."

Lani didn't say anything for a minute. When she did speak, it wasn't at all what he expected. "Would you like to walk with me on the beach?"

"It's a tempting offer, and I would accept it gladly if I didn't want to get this business with Anne McGregor out of the way." He struggled with impatience. "No more delays, Lani. Either Anne McGregor is here or she isn't. Either I see her tonight or I don't, but this cat-and-mouse game is over."

She turned toward the beach. "No more delays. If you'll come with me, I'll introduce you to Anne McGregor."

Since he had nothing to lose under the circumstances, he went with her. There was enough light from the tiki torches and the moon to enable them to see where they were walking. The sand gave under their feet, and this close to the ocean, the wind was strong without the buffer of trees and bushes. It pulled at the material of Lani's dress and tossed her hair around her face. Rhys didn't know where they were going, as he couldn't see any other house among the palm-tree-bordered shoreline. Oddly enough, now that they were on their way to meet the McGregor woman, he was no longer as impatient as he had been.

Near one of the torches, Lani stopped walking. She wanted to be able to see Rhys's face. The wind was cooler now that the sun had set, but she was too preoccupied to notice. "I don't know quite where to start."

"How about at the beginning? That's usually a good place. Or maybe even in the middle. Hell, at this point, I'll even be willing to listen to the end first and sort it out later."

She smiled briefly at his rueful humor, then lifted her chin. The best way to get an unpleasant duty out of the way, she told herself, was to do it.

"When I first met you," she said, "you introduced yourself as Rhys Jones, leaving out part of your name. I did the same thing."

"Is this leading somewhere I want to go?"

She held out her right hand. "I'm Anne McGregor."

Two

It didn't dawn on him right away what she said. He had been concentrating on the attractive picture she made with the ocean as a backdrop, the flickering flames from the torch high-lighting her hair and making her skin glow. When it filtered through his tired brain what she had announced, he asked crossly, "Is that supposed to be funny?"

She shook her head. "I find nothing even faintly amusing about being Anne McGregor, Mr. Jones." Now that she had started, she wanted it over with. "My full name is Anne Kapiolani Makena McGregor."

"What is this? Some kind of game of jerk the jerk around? If this is a local Hawaiian tradition of changing names to fit a situation, I don't care for it."

He didn't believe her! She didn't know whether to laugh or scream in frustration. "I didn't realize I was going to need identification as proof. As you can see"—she gestured at her close-fitting dress to indicate the lack of pockets—"I didn't bring a driver's license with me."

His gaze roamed over the material that clung to her hips and breasts. "There wouldn't be room," he murmured. "So I'm expected simply to take your word for it?"

"Well, it would be nice, but I suppose it's a bit much to ask. My father is Richard Stuyvesant McGregor from Beaconsfield, England. At least, that's where he was from when he knew my mother. Originally, his family was from Scotland. I can't tell you much else about him because he left Hawaii before I was born. My mother was Lahela Makena McGregor. She died when I was three years old. My grandmother raised me and was the one who insisted I never use the name Anne McGregor."

"Why not?"

She had just told him more than she had ever explained to anyone outside of her family, she thought with frustration, and he still wasn't satisfied. "Does it matter? You wanted to find Anne McGregor. I don't remember anything being said about needing to know her life story."

"Humor me. I think you owe me for wasting my time. You could have told me who you were when we were in Waikiki. It would have saved a great deal of time if you had."

"I also could have kept my identity from you tonight. It's what my grandmother wanted me to do." She took several steps away, then turned back to face him. "Richard McGregor is not a subject we like to talk about. He hurt my mother very badly by leaving her and her unborn child to return to England. You see, his aristocratic family disapproved of his marrying someone who wasn't British. Leaving the way he did didn't exactly endear him to my family, especially my grandmother. She would just as soon forget he ever existed. I've told you who I am. Now I would like to know what you want."

Rhys studied her carefully. She had given the right information about Richard McGregor. Either she was who she said she was, or she knew the real Anne McGregor well enough to know her history. It didn't make sense that she would go to the trouble of impersonating another woman. Unless she thought there might be something in it for her.

"There's no money involved, if that's what you're hoping," he said quietly, his gaze never leaving her face.

Her hands clenched into fists at her sides. She wanted to slug him. Instead, she had to settle for walking away. She stepped around him. "If that's what you think of me, we're through with this conversation."

His arm shot out, his fingers wrapping around her wrist, effectively stopping her. "We're not through yet."

"As far as I'm concerned we are." She jerked away from him and placed her hands on her hips. "How dare you accuse me of wanting money from you. You were the one who insisted on meeting Anne McGregor. I didn't come looking for you. I should have listened to my grandmother. She said anything connected with the McGregor name meant trouble. She didn't want me to tell you who I was, but no, I had to be curious. I should have left Anne McGregor where she was."

Rhys watched her during her tirade, seeing the flames of the torch catch the green fire of temper in her eyes. "Are you finished?" he asked, his voice deceptively calm.

"Not quite. Tell me what you want."

"It isn't what I want. It's what your father wants. I have something he wants to give you."

Lani dropped her hands to her sides. "I told you," she said, her voice cool, "I don't want anything. "Especially from Richard McGregor."

"Is that why you never answered the letters my partner sent to you?"

"What are you talking about? I never received any letters from your office. I never heard of Smythe, whatever, and Berkeley-Jones until today."

"Smythe, Pritchard and Jones," he corrected her automatically. "Trevor Pritchard is the one who sent the letters to you. Each of the envelopes had been opened and resealed. Someone had received them and read them. They were addressed to you. Brilliant deduction would conclude that you opened them, read them, and sent them back."

He was wrong. She hadn't seen the letters, but she knew who must have. Her grandmother's address would be the only one Richard McGregor would have after all these years.

The wind had picked up and blew her hair into a tousled frenzy around her face. Lifting her hand, she gathered a wad of hair to keep it out of her face. Her eyes widened in surprise when he again grasped her wrist.

"Leave it," he said.

She didn't want him to touch her, but she didn't shy away from him. Whenever there was physical contact between them, it affected her strangely, and she didn't know what to do about it. "Tell me what you want, Mr. Jones. Or what Richard McGregor wants. Or what the letters wanted."

"Let's make it Rhys instead of Mr. Jones. It will be easier for you to say while you argue with me." Realizing he still held her, he released her wrist and added, "I don't think you're in the mood to hear about the gift your father wants you to have."

"So now you believe I'm Anne McGregor?"

He ran his hand over the back of his neck. "I'm

so punchy, I'll believe anything right now if it will help get this over with."

She raised her brows. It wasn't particularly flattering for him to state he was eager to see the last of her. "All you have to do is give me whatever Mr. McGregor wants me to have, and you can trot off to your hotel."

"I don't have it with me. It's not something I could slip into a pocket."

"Now you've made me curious. What is it that's so important?"

For the first time since she had met him, he looked self-conscious. Continuing to rub the back of his neck, he mumbled, "It's a basket."

She gaped in astonishment. "A what?"

He hadn't liked saying it the first time. His irritation was apparent as he repeated, "A basket. Right before I left England, my partner handed me this box he said contained a basket and asked me to deliver it to Anne McGregor."

Lani bit her lip to try to keep from laughing. It didn't work. She made a choking sound, then gave up. Her laughter was free and natural. She couldn't help it. His scowling expression only added to her amusement.

When she finally caught her breath, she had to ask, "All this fuss is about a basket?"

Rhys didn't appreciate her laughter, although he could understand it. The idea of a basket as a gift was bizarre to him, too. It was one of the reasons he had resented Trevor asking him to do this little favor. He cursed silently. This would be a lot easier if his head wasn't splitting.

"As I understand it," he said, "your father was in a car accident several months ago. He's been in a convalescent hospital because he still needs medical attention. Part of the physical therapy has included making baskets to improve his finger dexterity and the strength in his hands. For some reason he wants you to have one of the baskets he's made, and he contacted my partner, Trevor Pritchard, who is his attorney. When my plans to have a holiday in Australia were finalized and included a stopover in Hawaii, Trevor asked me to personally deliver the basket."

Lani's amusement faded. "You're serious."

"Afraid so. I know it sounds weird, but apparently your father is serious. Trevor said Richard McGregor might be eccentric, but he's also a valued client."

"If this is some kind of joke, I don't think it's very funny."

"From what I've gathered from my partner, Richard McGregor hasn't lost his marbles, but we'll just have to take his word for it. I told Trevor I would see that you received the basket. Once I hand it over to you, I won't bother you again."

It was too late, Lani thought. He already bothered her more than was comfortable. Several large rocks squatted on the sand about ten feet away, and she headed for them. Sitting down on one, she looked out over the dark ocean. Knowing why Rhys had wanted to find her gave her little satisfaction. Her curiosity about her father had always been shoved into the back of her mind by her grandmother's refusal to discuss him. When she was younger, she had often thought about what he might be like and what she would feel or do if she ever heard from him. now he had finally contacted her in a roundabout way with the gift of a basket.

Reality didn't quite live up to her childhood expectations.

Rhys closed the distance between them in several long strides but didn't join her on the rock. He was afraid he wouldn't be able to stand up again once he sat down. Besides, it was best to stay a safe distance from her or he might do something incredibly stupid—like draw her down onto the sand with him.

Between the moonlight and the tiki torch, he was able to see her features. Her hair seemed darker as the breeze off the ocean tossed the silky tresses gently on her bare shoulders. His gaze lowered to the soft rise of her breasts above the colorful dress. The tips of his fingers felt oddly sensitized with the desire to stroke her tanned flesh.

There was a dreamy quality about the whole scene. Palm trees, sand, salty air, and the undulating sea made an exotic setting. He felt disoriented with the change in time and climate and the lack of sleep. All those conditions explained why he was falling under the spell of this woman, he told himself. He had thought he was past the stage of fantasizing about a woman, yet he was wondering what it would be like to feel her mouth under his, her slender frame against his hard body. The sandy beach beneath his feet would adjust to her curves as they lay together, absorbing the warmth of the sun-soaked sand and each other.

To distract himself from the urge to put his tantalizing thoughts into action, he asked, "Are you going to accept the basket?"

She turned her head to look at him. "After all these years, he suddenly wants to give me a basket? It doesn't make sense."

"Does it have to?"

His tone was reasonable, his words practical. She wasn't in the mood to be either. "He couldn't even contact me personally. He went through his lawyer's office," she murmured with a hint of bitterness.

He didn't want to see the haunting sadness in her eyes, or respond to it. "Your father is willing to make some sort of contact with you. I agree a basket isn't exactly a terrific idea of a get-acquainted offer. Perhaps he expects you to acknowledge his gift by writing to him first."

Lani's gaze returned to the ocean. "For what purpose?"

"It beats me." His concentration was not up to its usual efficient standards. The distraction of the wind teasing the fabric of her dress where it was slit partway up the side wasn't much help either. "It's been my experience that people's motives for doing certain things often make sense only to the one doing them."

"I feel like I've just stepped off a familiar road into unknown territory and don't know which way I should go. The man has ignored me since I was born. Twenty-seven years later, he sends me a basket. Obviously, I'm supposed to be thrilled. You travel halfway around the world to deliver this strange gift." Her hair blew across her face when she again turned to look at him. "I don't understand anyone's motives at the moment."

He reached out and swept her hair off her face, the back of his fingers caressing her cheek. "Would you understand my motives better if they became more basic?"

Her breath caught in her throat as his touch seared her skin. "Why do I feel I shouldn't ask what they are?"

He smiled, letting his knuckle graze her firm jawline, her slender throat. "Probably because you know it's not necessary. Some things don't need to be explained, just explored."

His low voice sent tingles up her spine. For a moment her eyes locked with his. She didn't look away when she felt him clasp her arms. He drew her to her feet to stand in front of him, only inches from his tall frame. Slowly, as though he was giving her a chance to resist, he lowered his head.

Her hands flattened against his chest as his lips caressed hers, but instead of pushing him away, her fingers clenched in his shirt. The ocean was a safe distance away, yet she was being swept under by a strong current of sensations. Waves of desire washed over her, leaving her adrift in an uncharted sea.

When his mouth eased its possessive claim on hers, she breathed his name. "This is crazy."

"That explains it," he drawled softly.

His teeth nipped at her bottom lip, coaxing her mouth to open. Her breath caressed his skin when she made a sound that was part protest and part pleasure. That sound inflamed his desire, and he took her mouth with a fierce hunger for the taste of her, feeding on her response as though he had been starving for a very long time. His arms captured her, and his hands slid down her back, pressing her hips into his.

The wind blew her hair across his face and neck, tantalizing his hot skin with feathery strokes. His tongue sought hers as he deepened the kiss and tightened his hold on her. Her body arched into his, and needs rose up inside him, stronger than he thought he could control. A husky groan escaped him as he broke away from her mouth.

Before he lost what was left of his mind, he loosened his grip on her hips, easing her away from him enough to gain his sanity. Gazing down into her dazed eyes, he murmured, "I want to drag you down onto the sand and make love to you. The only thing stopping me is the fact your family is only a stone's throw away."

Shock jolted through the haze of sensuality he

had woven around her, and Lani realized making love with him was what she wanted, too. It didn't matter that he was a man she had known for less than a day. Her pulse throbbed with the passion he had sparked deep inside her, weakening her, yet making her feel the strength of her femininity.

"We'd better get back," she said, chilled by the knowledge she wanted a man she didn't even know.

His hands dropped away from her. "I suppose we should before your mammoth cousin comes looking for you and finds me."

She smiled faintly. "That's as good a reason as any."

As she retraced their steps back up the beach he fell in beside her. Hating the need he felt to have some sort of contact with her, he reached for her hand, threading his fingers through hers.

Her head jerked around, her eyes questioning.

"So I don't get lost," he murmured.

She returned her attention to the footprints they had previously made in the sand, not commenting on his remark. The tide would come in in a few hours, she thought, and it would wash away all traces of their stroll in the moonlight. It would take more time for her to forget what had happened between them that night.

His quiet voice broke through the barrier of her thoughts. "When will I see you again?"

She didn't look at him. "I can pick the basket up at your hotel tomorrow if it's convenient."

"Are you doing that on purpose?" he asked, tamping down his anger.

This time she did glance up. "Doing what?"

"Putting our relationship back on a business level."

She stopped walking and faced him. The planes of his face appeared hard and uncompromising in the shadowy light. Her instincts told her he was angry but didn't tell her why. "We don't have a relationship, Mr. Jones. We're barely acquaintances."

His fingers tightened around her hand as he tugged on her arm, bringing her against his hard body. "We have something, Lani. And it has nothing to do with the damn basket your father sent you. Now, when can I see you again?"

It wasn't in her nature to back down from a confrontation. Growing up with a number of aggressive male cousins had taught her to defend herself and to meet any challenge thrown at her. "When are you leaving the island?"

Disconcerted by her question, he took a moment to answer. "I have an open ticket to Australia. I didn't know how long it would take to find you."

"You've found me. There's no reason for you to stay in Hawaii any longer, is there?"

Lifting his free hand, he touched her jaw before sliding his fingers along her neck to her nape. Satisfaction flowed through him when he saw her lashes flicker and her eyes glaze over with sensual longing. "Isn't there?" he asked softly.

She shook her head as if to clear it. "No, there isn't. I'm not part of the island's tourist attractions to be used and discarded before you get back on the airplane. I'll take the basket you've come to deliver. Then your duty will have been done, and our association will be over. I can't put it any clearer than that."

His fingers combed through her hair, letting it fall onto her bare shoulders. "That's fairly clear, all right. You left out one little thing."

She frowned. "What's that?"

Watching her carefully, he trailed his hand over her shoulder, then stroked one finger across the rise of her breasts. His faint smile held a hint of male triumph as he heard her quick intake of breath, and he dipped his finger beneath her dress.

Rhys quickly realized that what had started out as an example of how she reacted to his touch, was turning into a lesson on how weak his control was when he touched her. The tip of his finger grazed the hardening bud of her breast. He saw her eyelashes lower to cover her expressive eyes, and her lips part as her breathing quickened.

"Lani, look at me."

Slowly, she did as he asked. "Rhys, stop."

He found the answer he wanted in the depths of her green eyes. "That's the problem. I don't want to stop." He withdrew his finger reluctantly. "But I have to. This isn't the time or the place." Placing his hand under her chin, he tilted her head up so he could see her face better. "You might not be willing to admit it, but you want me. I can see it in your eyes and feel it when I touch you."

She didn't bother to lie to him. "It doesn't matter. You're on the island for a short time, and I'm not interested in warming your bed while you're here."

His brain told him she was right. It was his body that was giving him an argument. He drew his thumb across her bottom lip. "We'll discuss it during the drive back to Waikiki."

Lani didn't agree or disagree. She was learning he heard what he wanted to hear. What he had yet to learn was she also had her own way of doing things.

Apparently he didn't expect an argument since he went ahead to ask another question. "You said this was your grandmother's house. Do you live here with her?"

"No," she replied with a breath of a laugh, starting to walk again. "I don't live with Tutu. I have a cottage in Waianae that belongs to one of my cousins."

"Do you work around here?"

She shook her head. "In Honolulu."

Remembering the length of time it took to get from Waikiki to Makaha, he commented, "That's quite a drive to make every day. What do you do?"

"I work in a bank."

He stopped walking. "A bank?"

She chuckled. "Yes, a bank. Why are you so surprised?"

He resumed walking. "I don't know. This has been a day full of surprises. You would think I would be used to them by now. It's just that I can't picture you behind a teller's window."

"You don't need to because I'm not behind a teller's window. I deal with foreign-currency exchanges." She caught his expression and smiled. "I've read about people looking thunderstruck. This is the first time I've ever seen it."

"Too bad you don't have a camera. Why a bank?"

"Why not? It pays well enough. I have my evenings and weekends free."

"Why am I getting the impression your work is not a very significant part of your life?"

"It's a job," she replied with a shrug.

Her attitude was the exact opposite of his own, he mused. His work was the most important thing in his life. Practicing law was all he had ever wanted to do. It was his vocation, his hobby, his mistress, and his life's blood. And because he put everything he had into it, he was the victim of migraines.

He rubbed the back of his neck to ease the dull ache. It had become an automatic gesture over the last couple of months, and he wasn't even aware of it.

Lani was, though. She figured the action could

simply be a habit, or it could be caused by something else. Perhaps exhaustion.

As they approached the grassy area of Emma's
property, they left behind the peace and serenity
of the beach. The group was still playing guitars
and drums and singing. A baby was crying. Doz-
ens of adults were talking and laughing and eating.

A number of children ran up to Lani and tugged
at her hands. Since they were all talking at once,
she couldn't tell what they were saying.

She held up her hand. "One at a time. Luka,
you tell me what's going on."

A boy with long black hair spoke up. "Auntie
Lia said to come get you. They want to bring out
Tutu's birthday cake."

"All right. I'm coming."

She didn't immediately follow the children as
they ran off. Rhys saw her hesitate and said, "Go
ahead. I can fend for myself."

"All right."

As she walked toward the house her gaze searched
for Kimo. When she saw him and had caught his
attention, she gave an abrupt nod of her head
before entering the house.

Rhys decided to find an extremely uncomfortable place to sit to wait for Lani. Perhaps, he
thought, he could find an iron chair or a bench
with nails in it. One or the other might be effec-
tive in keeping him awake. All things considered,
it had been an extremely interesting night, so he
shouldn't complain because it wasn't going to end
quite yet. He couldn't ignore the signs of an on-
coming migraine—the tightness in his neck, the
white spots in front of his eyes.

He slipped his hand into a pocket in his slacks,
and his fingers closed around a small plastic bottle of medication. He waged a minor battle with
himself before releasing the bottle. The doctor's

instructions had been to take a pill at the onset of a headache, but the pills knocked him out. His smile held a trace of self-mockery as he thought of Lani's reaction to finding him passed out under a palm tree. It wasn't the impression he preferred to make.

It would help if he could keep his eyes open. He leaned against the rough trunk of a palm tree. Something caught his attention about twenty yards away from where he was standing. His eyes narrowed as he focused on a white object swaying in the breeze between two trees. It wasn't a feather bed, but it would do.

The hammock rocked as he collapsed into it. The woven rope closed around him, and his eyes closed. He would rest for a few minutes. Just a couple of minutes. His head was beginning to ache with a vengeance, and the dots in front of his eyes were becoming balloons. He didn't want to resort to the little pills the doctor had prescribed, not if he could get by without them.

The next thing he knew, someone was shaking his shoulder. Opening his eyes to narrow slits, he saw Kimo bending over him.

"Hello, mate. I've missed you," Rhys drawled with dry amusement. "Is it your turn for guard duty?"

Kimo blinked in surprise. "I'm going to drive you back to your hotel."

It was not a good idea to argue with a mountain, but Rhys gave it a try. "Thanks anyway. I'm waiting for Lani."

"She'll be a while. I have a show to do in Waikiki, so I was going there anyway. It'll save Lani the drive back."

Logistically, it made sense, except that Rhys would rather spend an hour on the road with Lani than with Kimo. If his exhausted brain hadn't turned to mush, he might have been able to come up with a darned good reason why Kimo should toddle off to Waikiki by himself.

Instead he asked curiously, "What kind of show?"

"I do a nightclub act at Trader Vic's."

Rhys could picture Kimo as a bouncer in a nightclub, but not as an entertainer. "What kind of act do you do?"

"I dance. Play drums. Sing."

The mind boggled. No matter how hard he tried, Rhys couldn't visualize the large man dancing on stage, unless he held a spear in one hand and a club in the other. Feeling he should say something, he murmured, "I see," although he really couldn't.

"It's too bad you're going to be leaving the island," Kimo said. "You might have enjoyed stopping by one evening."

There was something wrong with the man's statement, but Rhys was too tired to figure it out. He couldn't come up with whatever it was at the moment. It was something to do with his leaving the island. His eyes shut. His headache was becoming more severe. He would think about it later.

Kimo reached down, planting a huge hand on Rhys's shoulder, and gave it another shove. Nothing. No reaction at all. Shaking his head, Kimo walked back to the house.

He found Lani serving slices of birthday cake. Pulling her aside, he said, "I can't deliver your package to Waikiki like you wanted."

"Why not?"

"I can't wake it up."

She pulled him away from the others in case they were overheard. "What do you mean you can't wake him up?"

"He's passed out in the hammock. I guess he had too many wine coolers."

She shook her head. "He only had one and I never even saw him take a sip. He said he hadn't had any sleep for what seemed like a month. He's evidently exhausted from traveling. England isn't exactly a couple of miles away." Under her breath, she muttered, "Damn. What do we do with him now? If we leave him in the hammock, Tutu will throw him to the sharks when she finds him in the morning."

"Make up your mind. I have to get to the club."

There were only two choices. One was she could ask Kimo to deliver Rhys, awake or not, to his hotel room before he went on to the club. It would be the practical thing to do. Oddly enough, it wasn't the choice she made.

Three

Rhys slowly came out of the heavy fog of sleep and opened his eyes. He closed them and opened them again. Instead of palm trees and a hammock, he was surrounded by four walls and was lying in a soft bed. He hadn't spent much time in his hotel room, but still knew this wasn't it.

Propping himself up against a brass headboard, he looked around. Opposite the bed was a dresser with several bottles of perfume and a black lacquer jewelry box in the center of its polished top. A cooling breeze came through the louvered windows near him, ruffling lace curtains. There was a rattan chair in the corner with a robe draped over the arm. A woman's robe. This definitely wasn't his hotel room.

The last thing he remembered was Kimo hovering over the hammock, glowering down at him and saying something about taking him back to his hotel. Unless Kimo wore feminine apparel—which was extremely doubtful—this wasn't the large man's bedroom either.

Where the hell was he? he wondered as he lifted

the sheet and looked down. And where was his clothes? He somehow had lost his pants and his shirt. And evidently his mind.

Tossing back the sheet, he flung his feet over the side of the bed. On the bedside table, he saw a small clock. He reached over and turned it so he could see the time. It was a little after two o'clock. Apparently two in the afternoon, since the sun was shining brightly outside. He knew the when. Now all he had to figure out was the where and how.

His slacks and shirt were folded and stacked on another chair on the far side of the room. He put them on, then went into the adjoining bathroom and splashed water on his face. Opening the medicine cabinet above the sink he saw a razor on the bottom shelf. He had to make do with soap instead of shaving cream, but it was better than nothing. He would have liked to take a shower and put on clean clothes, but that would have to wait until he returned to the hotel.

Leaving the bathroom and bedroom, he entered a small living room furnished with a bamboo couch and chair with colorful cushions done in a white and green fern print. There were several bamboo tables, a wall unit that contained a stereo and a small television, along with books neatly arranged among figurines. The paintings on the walls depicted island scenes and went well with the view of the ocean out a large picture window. On a table against an inner wall was an aquarium with a pump bubbling away. Greenery was artfully arranged on the bottom, and a plastic sunken pirate ship was partially buried in the colorful gravel. From where he stood he couldn't see any fish swimming around. Stepping closer, he bent down and peered through the glass. Darting in and out of the seaweed-type plants were sea horses, about an inch high. For several minutes, he watched them in fascination, until he realized he had more important things to do. Like finding out where in blazes he was.

The only other room was the kitchen. It was as empty of people as the other rooms. He could have mortgaged his soul for a cup of coffee, but he was out of luck. A quick but thorough search of the cupboards didn't reveal either a coffeepot or the necessary coffee grounds. The doctor was going to get his way again. Caffeine wasn't considered one of the things he should have.

He took a bottle of juice from the refrigerator and poured himself a glass. Since his host, whoever he or she was, was conspicuously absent, he couldn't very well ask permission before helping himself. Leaning his hip against the counter, he drank deeply. The peach-colored liquid had an unusual but pleasant taste. It didn't have the kick of caffeine, but its flavor, unlike any other juice he had ever had, was delicious.

He examined the room, hoping to come up with some kind of clue as to who occupied the house. Everything looked like normal furnishings for a kitchen—except for the long rectangular glass aquarium on the table in front of a window. The sides were about six inches high, and he could see there was water in the bottom, a few rocks set into it. After the sea horses in the living room, he was curious to see what kind of creature was in this.

Carrying the juice with him, he walked over to the table and looked down. Behind one of the larger rocks, he saw a turtle sitting on a flat stone. Its shell was about five inches from bow to stern, its head poking out as it munched contentedly on what looked like a piece of lettuce.

Shaking his head as though the action would

clear his brain, Rhys returned to his previous position at the counter, feeling more disoriented than ever.

The creaking of the spring on the screen door had him turning his head. Lani entered, and his breath caught in his throat. Her hair was wind-blown, a mass of waves and soft curls. She wore a soft cotton T-shirt in a delicate shade of peach. It was a couple of sizes too big, with the sleeves rolled up several turns. White cuffed shorts emphasized the tanned length of her legs and she was barefoot. In her arms she carried a clump of green bananas.

"Hello," she said as she set them on the counter. "Feeling better?"

"I feel like I'm only two time zones behind instead of five." Holding up the glass, he added, "I hope you don't mind. I helped myself to some juice."

She tore a banana off the bunch and began peeling it. "No problem. Would you like something to eat?"

"I'd like an explanation first. Where am I, and how did I get here?"

"This is my home, and Kimo brought you. You were completely out of it." She smiled. "He thought you had one too many wine coolers."

'I wish," Rhys mumbled irritably.

She continued peeling bananas. "I explained you were suffering from a bad case of jet lag."

She didn't mention the bottle of medication that had fallen out of his slacks when she was folding them, after Kimo had tugged them off the supine figure on her bed. She had read the label and discovered Rhys was being treated for migraines. It explained why he had rubbed the back of his neck a number of times, and why she had seen pain in the depths of his eyes.

"Why did your cousin bring me here?" Rhys asked as she cut the bananas in half lengthwise and placed them in a frying pan with a pat of butter.

"He didn't like the idea of dragging you through the lobby of your hotel, so I suggested he drag you here instead. We couldn't very well leave you in Tutu's hammock."

"I got the impression your grandmother doesn't care for me much. Is that why you didn't introduce us?"

"It isn't you exactly," she murmured.

"What is it exactly?"

"You're English, and the reason you came to the islands has to do with Richard McGregor. Those are two strikes against you."

He set his empty glass on the counter and closed the distance between them. Placing his fingers under her chin, he turned her head so she had to look at him. "Do you have the same prejudices?"

"If I did, I would never have brought you to the luau or have Kimo put you in my bed," she said bluntly.

His thumb stroked her soft cheek. "Speaking of your bed, where did you sleep last night?"

"The couch." She turned her head, halting his disturbing caress. She hadn't imagined her reaction to his touch the day before, she thought. During the night she had convinced herself it had been her imagination. "I have to flip these or they'll burn."

Rhys dropped his hand. It was proving more and more difficult to allow her to keep pushing him away. "Who undressed me? You or Kimo?"

"Kimo. He thought you might be uncomfortable sleeping in your clothes."

Rhys was disappointed. The thought of her removing his clothing held intriguing possibilities.

However, when and if she ever did strip off his clothes, he wanted to be awake.

"You wouldn't happen to have any coffee, would you?"

"Sorry. I don't drink coffee." She removed the fried bananas from the pan and set them on a plate, then walked over to the small table in front of the window. "I thought you British preferred tea."

"Not exclusively. What can I do to help?"

"You can set the table."

Showing he was no slouch in the kitchen, he found the plates, silverware, and cloth napkins without any difficulty and arranged them on the table.

Raising a brow, she commented, "I'm impressed."

He looked up. "What about?"

"I don't know many men who know how to set a table correctly. Kimo sort of piles everything in one spot and expects everyone to grab what they need."

"One of the jobs I had to help finance my education was as a waiter in a posh restaurant."

"One of them? How many jobs did you have?"

"I never took the time to count them." They had been a means to an end. He preferred to forget them. He finished setting the table, then asked, "How about you? Have you always worked in a bank?"

"It seems like I've worked there forever. I started out as a teller, and I was promoted two years ago."

His gaze was curious. "No aspirations for more, like president of the bank?"

"None. It's a job, that's all. I like the people I work with and the work I do is interesting enough to keep me from getting bored." She couldn't read his expression, although she sensed he thought her attitude strange. "Not ambitious enough for you?"

For several moments he didn't answer. Then he gave her a half smile. "Perhaps your thinking is more sensible than mine. I work fourteen hours a day seven days a week. My work is just about all I think about. Even when I leave the office, I don't leave the work behind. I either take paperwork home or I'm thinking about one case or the other."

"Which might be why you have to take those pills," she said quietly.

Anger flickered in his eyes. "Been picking my pockets, Miss Makena?"

"The prescription bottle fell out of your pants pocket when I was draping the pants over a chair." Her smile was a trifle self-conscious. "I sort of read the label."

"Then you sort of know what they're for," he said dryly. If it had been up to him, he wouldn't have told her about his affliction. Since she knew about it, he admitted. "The headaches have been getting worse and more frequent, which is why I'm on holiday."

She tilted her head slightly as she studied him. "How long has it been since you've taken a vacation?"

"This is my first." He considered the damn headaches a weakness, and he wasn't the type of man who took kindly to having any weaknesses. He saw her frown and shake her head in puzzlement. "What?"

She shrugged. "It's just that I've never known anyone whose whole life revolved around his job. We're a little more laid back here. We believe in working for a living, but there's so much more to living than being forever behind a desk buried in paperwork. I can't imagine giving up my friends, not being able to be with my family, or to go to the ocean while the sun is shining. It appears to me you should be thinking of changing your priorities."

"There's a rather pompous doctor in Harley Street in London who would agree with you." Changing the subject, he asked, "Do I set a place for your friend?"

She blinked. "Who?"

He tapped the side of the shallow aquarium, drawing the attention of its occupant. The turtle turned his head in the direction of the sound. "This friend."

Grinning, Lani came over to the table and reached into the aquarium. She lifted the turtle out by grasping each side of the hard shell, then rested it on her palm.

"This is Tommy," she said, extending her hand to Rhys.

He blinked. "Tommy?"

"What would you call a turtle?"

"I haven't a clue." She was clearly expecting him to do something with the turtle. "If it was a dog, I would pet it. If it was a cat, I would scratch its neck. I'll be damned if I know what to do with a turtle."

She placed her forefinger under the turtle's head and gently caressed its lower jaw and throat. The turtle responded by extending his head out even farther. Rhys found himself copying her by reaching out to stroke the turtle in the same way, surprised that the skin was soft and supple.

"Wouldn't he be happier doing whatever turtles do naturally, rather than be in captivity?"

"He's blind. I found him one morning on the beach. Evidently he was washed ashore and couldn't find his way back to the water. I watched him for about an hour until it finally occurred to me he couldn't see. I took him to a vet and learned I was right. There was no way for the vet to determine what had caused the blindness. It could have been from birth, an injury, or a disease. He would die if he was returned to the wild."

Rhys watched as she carefully set the turtle on the flat rock in the aquarium. Would she ever stop surprising him? he wondered. He felt slightly dazed, as though he had ventured into a land more foreign than any country he could name. He couldn't envision any other woman he knew keeping sea horses or taking care of a handicapped turtle. As he had already figured out, Lani was not like anyone else. And he had never wanted a woman more than he craved her.

It took only a few minutes for her to finish preparing the rest of their lunch, which consisted of a platter of cold chicken and a fruit salad to go with the fried bananas. She brought the pitcher of juice and two glasses to the table. He held her chair for her, then sat down across from her.

"What have you been doing while I was snoozing away in your bed?" he asked.

"Nothing exciting. I tidied up the house, did some washing, and went for a swim. You didn't miss much."

Except, he thought, he could have been with her instead of wasting time sleeping. He cut a small piece of the fried banana, eyeing it warily. Sensing her gaze on him, he ate it, finding it surprisingly good.

"I've never eaten a fried banana before."

"Really? I would never have guessed. I'm completely out of kippers, so you'll have to make due with our island fare."

He made a face. "I don't fancy kippers much. I usually make do with coffee for breakfast."

"Since it's afternoon, I would call this more of a lunch than a breakfast." She picked up her glass and took a sip of juice. "Tell me about London. Is it really foggy all the time like in the movies?"

"You must watch some very old movies. There is the occasional foggy morning, but nothing like it used to be when everyone had coal fires to heat their homes. The smoke used to hang over London like a gray blanket."

"Have you always lived there?"

He shook his head. "I was born and raised in Denham, a small town northeast of London. My mother had a tea shop there until she retired. Now she lives in Australia. I bought her a small cottage five years ago where she tends to her roses and bakes more cakes than any ten people could eat comfortably in a lifetime. I have a flat in Bayswater. That's in London."

That explained why he was going to Australia, Lani mused, although she was curious why his mother had emigrated there. "What about your father?"

"He was a postman. He died when I was eight, so I don't remember much about him except he smoked a rather smelly pipe and soaked his feet in a basin of water every night." He rested his arms on the table and leaned toward her. "Why all the questions?"

"Just making conversation."

He sat back in his chair, smiling. "How disappointing. I was hoping you were asking all those questions because you wanted to know more about me."

"For what purpose? You'll be leaving in a couple of days, maybe sooner."

His gaze drifted over her tanned face and tousled hair. She wore no makeup and hadn't bothered tidying her hair or dressing up just because she had a guest. She didn't need any artificial aids to add to her beauty. She was as natural and as exotic as the food she had served for lunch.

"Maybe not," he said softly.

Lani felt uncomfortable under his steady gaze. She couldn't help feeling he saw more than she wanted him to see. "Maybe not what?"

"Maybe I'm not leaving the island as soon as you think."

"I thought you were on your way to Australia."

"I am. Eventually. After the travelog I received from your cousins, I have a feeling I'm missing a great deal by not taking in the sights and sounds of the island while I'm here. It would help if I had a guide to show me around, someone who knew Hawaii."

"The hotel can arrange for a tour guide, if that's what you want."

Shaking his head, he gave her one of his rare smiles. "You aren't going to make it easy, are you? You know I meant you."

His smile did odd things to her breathing and sent the blood racing through her veins. "You should do that more often."

He looked puzzled. "Do what? Ask you to take me around the island?"

"No, smile. You have a very nice smile, you know. It's a shame not to use it more." She gathered up her plate and cutlery. As she stood she added, "I've never met anyone as serious as you."

He was disconcerted by her remarks and wasn't sure how to respond to them. "International law is a serious business."

"We aren't discussing international law."

"That's true. We were discussing you showing me around the island."

She carried her dishes over to the sink. "Sorry. I work tomorrow. You'll have to find someone else if you're serious about wanting to see the island."

She heard his chair scrape on the floor. A few seconds later he was standing beside her. When she reached for the faucet, he took her hand and turned her toward him.

"I'm very serious, Lani. I want to see you again. I need to see you again."

She looked up at him, stunned by the heat in his eyes. She was saved from answering by the sound of a horn. "That's Kimo. He's going to drive you into Waikiki."

He didn't release her hand. "Why can't you drive me back?"

"Kimo has a show to do this afternoon in Waikiki. He offered to take you."

Feeling as though he was grasping at a very thin straw, Rhys asked, "What about the present from your father? If you drove me to my hotel, you could pick up the gift at the same time."

"You can give it to Kimo. I can get it from him later."

His fingers tightened around her small hand. "No," he said with irritation. "I'll only give it to you. You'll just have to come and get it."

The horn blasted several more times. "You'd better go. It wouldn't be a good idea to keep Kimo waiting."

Rhys realized the last thing he needed was to make her large cousin cross. Lowering his head, he took her mouth abruptly, crushing her lips under his, needing to take her taste with him.

For a moment the world disappeared as she responded to his hunger. Then the sound of the horn honking again intruded.

Raising his head, Rhys looked at her for a long moment. "I'll see you later," he said. Then he left.

Early Monday morning, Lani tapped on the door

of Rhys's hotel room several times without getting any results. She glanced at her watch. Seven-thirty. She knocked louder. The chances were good that Rhys was still in bed, but she wanted to get this over with before she went to work.

With her fist, she pounded heavily on the door, loud enough to wake the dead. When she stopped, she heard a muted voice that became clearer as Rhys neared the door. It was odd, she thought, how refined curses sounded in a British accent.

The door was yanked open and Rhys growled, "What the bloody hell do—" He stopped abruptly, and for a few seconds he simply stared at her.

Lani was just as startled at the sight of him. His hair was mussed, his eyes squinting as though the light hurt them. He had put on a pair of jeans, although the top button was still undone, and he hadn't bothered putting on a shirt. His jeans surprised her. The few times she had seen him, he had been dressed in more formal clothing. The immaculate man she had met two days ago had completely disappeared, replaced by a slightly disheveled grumpy man who needed a shave.

All her life she had seen men in various stages of nudity. In the islands shorts were standard attire. So why would the sight of Rhys's bare chest create such a strange yearning in her—a yearning to see the rest of him without the civilized trappings of his clothes? It was a question that had only one answer. She was physically attracted to the man. It was that simple and that complicated.

"Good morning," she murmured weakly.

He grabbed her arm and pulled her into his room. "I was prepared to do bodily harm to who-ever was hammering on my door. I've changed my mind."

"I'm pleased to hear it. And I'm sorry to wake

you. I thought I would pick up the basket before I went to work. That way you can go on to Australia with a free conscience."

A muscle clenched in his jaw, and he ran his free hand over his eyes. "You didn't happen to bring any coffee, did you?"

It wasn't the reaction she had expected. "Sorry. I always seem to be apologizing because I don't have any coffee. I do have a solution, however. This is a first-class hotel. They have room service."

His gaze roamed over her, from her hair tamed into a neat coil, her royal blue shirtwaist dress cinched at the waist with a wide belt, down to her matching blue heels. "You look different," he stated, sounding as if he wasn't sure he liked what he saw.

"I told you. I'm on my way to work. I can't very well wear a pareau to the bank."

"What a shame."

He began to walk toward the bedroom, pulling her along. Lani stumbled after him, too surprised to protest. Until he sat on the bed.

"Now wait a minute," she said, her heart thudding hard at the thought of sharing his bed. "What do you think you're doing?"

He tugged on her arm, forcing her down beside him, before he reached for the phone on the bedside table. Stabbing out several numbers, he said, "I'm ordering coffee."

That explained what he was doing, she thought, but not why she had to be with him while he did it. "You can't do that by yourself?"

"It's more friendly this way. Besides, this way I know you'll stay." He ordered a pot of coffee, giving his room number before hanging up. When he turned to her, he asked casually, "Did I say good morning?"

She blinked in confusion. "No, I don't think so."

Suddenly she found herself on her back on top of his rumpled sheets, his body partially covering hers. She could feel the rough material of his jeans against her leg as he propped himself up on one elbow.

The look he gave her was warm and intimate. "Good morning."

"Good morning," she responded automatically, slightly alarmed at how breathless the two words came out.

His own voice was husky with sleep. "Where is the sexy lady who danced the hula in a provocative dress?"

"I left her at home along with the dress."

"Pity." He ran his finger down the open neck of her dress, stopping his progress at the top button. "Not that I don't find this Lani equally desirable. It's just that you have more clothes on today than yesterday."

"I can't wear shorts to the bank either."

He smiled. "You'd certainly have a lot more customers if you did."

"Would you let me up, please?"

He shook his head slowly. "Now why would I want to do that? I crawled into this bed thinking about you, had trouble falling asleep in this bed because of you, so why would I let you off this bed now that you're here?"

"Because I asked you to?" she said hopefully.

Lowering his head, he brushed his lips over hers. "I'm afraid that won't do it. If I can't have coffee to wake me up, I'll have you."

"You can't have me."

"Why not?"

She said the only thing that came to her mind. "I don't have time. I have to go to work."

"How much time do you have?"

"Time enough for a handshake, a basket, and a good-bye."

Rhys examined the fine lines of her face and the golden lights in her green eyes as she met his gaze. He would give her the basket, but not the handshake. Nor would he say good-bye.

He cupped her cheek in his hand. "I want more than that from you."

"For all I know, there could be a Mrs. Berkeley-Jones."

"There is."

She stiffened, shock widening her eyes, and attempted to push him away.

"Take it easy," he said with amusement. "The only Mrs. Jones who is related to me is my mother. I told you about her yesterday."

"Oh," she breathed.

He lowered his gaze to her lips, which were slightly parted and inviting. He had to have her mouth again, to see if he had imagined the taste of her. Need exploded through him as he heard her quick intake of breath when he touched her lips with his. Deepening the kiss, his tongue sought the intimate warmth of her.

Lani went rigid under him as she fought the riot of sensations exploding through her. She clenched the cool sheet to keep from putting her arms around him to hold him closer. She could stop her hands from touching him but couldn't prevent her response to the magic of his devastating kiss.

He left her mouth to find her delicate neck. When his fingers began to loosen the first button on her dress, she closed her hand around his wrist.

Softly, she murmured one word. "No."

He raised his head, his blue eyes warmly sensual as he looked down at her. He knew stopping was going to be extremely difficult, but it was what he had to do. He kissed her quickly before levering his long body off her and the bed. "I don't suppose you would wait around until I've showered and then have a cup of coffee with me?"

She shook her head. "I don't have time."

A corner of his mouth curved upward. "I didn't think so. I'm beginning to dislike that word *time*."

He walked over to the dresser and opened one of the drawers. After taking out a shirt, he looked back to where she still lay on the bed. "It would greatly assist my act of chivalry if you would get off the bed, Lani. It wouldn't take much for me to rejoin you."

Lani sat up and watched him shrug into a shirt. That helped a little, but not enough. During the long night and the drive that morning to Waikiki, she had told herself she had imagined the attraction between them. She put it down to the unusual way they had met and the shock of hearing about her father after all these years. The hard-fought rationalization didn't help her now.

She got off the bed and walked into the living room of the suite. The intimate atmosphere of his bedroom was more than she needed right now. Looking at her watch, she saw she had used up fifteen minutes of the time she had allotted. She glanced around the room, hoping to find the darn basket so she could get out of there. Before she said or did something she would regret later.

All she could see were the usual hotel furnishings—tables and chairs, and a love seat and sofa covered with a colorful Hawaiian print. There was no sign of Rhys in this room as there had been in his bedroom. It was a typical hotel suite, bright and cheerful with a large window overlooking the ocean.

Going over to the window, she gazed out at the turquoise water. She didn't look at the tourists on the beach or swimming in the sea. Instead, she studied the water she had seen all her life, wondering why it appeared different today.

"You look like you'd rather be out on the beach than cooped up in a bank."

Turning her head, she saw Rhys standing in the arched doorway of his bedroom. His shirt was tucked in at his slim waist, his hands jammed into his jeans pockets. "There's nothing stopping you from enjoying the ocean," she said, "or is your flight leaving today?"

He leaned against the doorframe. "I'd rather wait until you get off work. Then you can join me."

She smiled. "You don't give up, do you?"

"You might want to remember that," he said quietly.

His eyes drilled into her, his expression serious. Then, abruptly, he disappeared back into the bedroom. In twenty seconds he returned, carrying a medium-sized box that he brought over to her. She accepted it, but didn't open it.

"Don't you want to see what it looks like?" he asked.

"I'll wait until I get home tonight."

Since there was no reason for her to stay, she walked toward the door, half expecting him to stop her. He didn't say a word. Shifting the package to one arm, she opened the door.

Without looking at him, she said, "It was my grandmother who opened the letters from your office and sent them back. She won't apologize for any inconvenience she's caused you or your partners, so I will for her." Glancing over her shoulder, she added, "She was only trying to protect me. I'll send a thank-you note to Richard McGregor to the address on the business card you gave me. It will be up to your office to send it on to him."

"I'll see that it's done."

She nodded. "All right. Thanks. Aloha, Rhys Berkeley-Jones. It's been . . . interesting meeting you."

He hadn't moved from his position, nor did he respond to her farewell speech. His arms were loosely crossed over his chest as he watched her with that intense gaze.

Disconcerted by his lack of response, Lani tightened her grip on the box and walked out of his suite, closing the door softly behind her.

She quickened her step toward the elevator, feeling oddly deflated at his apparent lack of interest in the fact that he would never be seeing her again. Regret and disappointment lay heavily on her as she rode the elevator down to the lobby.

After the door closed, Rhys slowly walked over to the window, standing where Lani had stood a moment ago. He hadn't had nearly enough sleep to make up for all the hours of rest he had missed, despite the sleep he had had at Lani's cottage, but he didn't return to his bed.

His mouth curved into a faint smile as he remembered his partner's reaction to his phone call. It had given him great pleasure to shock Trevor, as he had when he'd placed a call to London after returning to his room the previous day. Before he had left England, he had told his partners he would take the time off everyone was insisting he take, but only if he could combine business with pleasure. An Australian company was involved in litigation with their firm. By talking with the representatives in person, he might be able to settle the suit out of court.

When he'd spoken to Trevor, he had reported mission accomplished on the Basket Case, as he sarcastically referred to it, then added he was going to stay in Hawaii longer than he had originally planned. He would take care of the litigation matter by phone if necessary. He had also phoned his mother to tell her he was going to be delayed a few days. He didn't explain why, though he knew the reason himself.

He was going to find out what it was about Lani that made him grind his teeth with irritation and ache with the need to bury himself deep inside her. He was becoming obsessed with the woman. She had to be exorcised from his mind and body or he would never be free of her.

He laughed aloud, though without amusement. The doctor had given him strict instructions to rest. There was nothing restful about his attraction to Anne Kapiolani Makena McGregor.

Four

Rhys left his hotel room in plenty of time to be at Lani's bank before she left for the day. Using the telephone book provided by the hotel, he had found the bank's number. Calling there, he'd learned what time they closed. The helpful hotel clerk had called a taxi for him, which delivered him in front of the bank fifteen minutes before closing time.

He didn't know how long she worked after the bank was closed to the public, but that wasn't a problem. He would simply wait.

Two men were standing on either side of the bank entrance like sentinels, although they were casually dressed in aloha shirts and white slacks. They bore more than a striking resemblance to Lani's overly healthy cousin, causing Rhys to give them a second look. Their physiques were similar, though both were shorter. Since they wore sunglasses, he wasn't able to tell if they were looking at him or not.

After the less-than-subtle warning Kimo had delivered during the drive back to his hotel the day before, Rhys wouldn't be too surprised if Kimo had arranged for a couple of friends or relatives to keep an eye on Lani. Or he was becoming paranoid.

He spotted a place to wait where he could see the entrance of the bank yet be out of the way of the people going in and out. He leaned against a mailbox and slipped on a pair of dark glasses. He hadn't gotten used to the brilliant colors of the island. It wasn't just the bright sun. The sky, the trees, the flowers, the clothing, the people were all an explosion of vibrant colors.

He was beginning to think his doctor was right about insisting he go on holiday. Years of working had taken a greater toll than he'd thought. He hadn't known what it felt like to relax until he had come to the island. Breathing in the clear air with the sun warming his skin, he could feel his nerve endings slacken.

A police car raced by with its siren screaming and lights flashing. About a block away, the car screeched to a halt. Two policeman jumped out and ran into a building. Rhys watched the action along with most of the others on the street.

When he turned back to face the bank again, he wasn't able to see the entrance because the two Kimo clones were standing directly in front of him. Neither one spoke. They just simply looked at him, an unspoken threat in their stance and intimidating expression.

Crossing his arms across his chest, he said quietly, "If you're going to ask for directions, I'm afraid I can't help you."

The strap of Lani's bag slipped off her shoulder as she pushed open the glass door. It seemed appropriate, considering the way she was feeling —as though her mind had degenerated into a mass of jelly. Wherever her mind had gone, it certainly hadn't been on her work.

She shifted the cumbersome box to one arm so she could pull the strap back onto her shoulder. As the bank door closed behind her she sighed with pleasure. The fresh air and sunshine were what she badly needed after eight hours in an air-conditioned building. She wondered what was wrong with her. Depression had dragged at her all day, no matter how hard she'd tried to push it away. It wasn't like her to be restless and edgy—or preoccupied with thoughts of a man, to the exclusion of everything else.

She tightened her grasp on the box Rhys had given her and turned toward the parking lot, then stopped abruptly when she saw two of her cousins. Her surprise wasn't due to seeing her relatives. It was who they were talking to that made her suddenly worry.

They weren't just chatting, though. Unless intimidation could be classified as talking. And she could tell by all three men's aggressive stances, they weren't discussing the weather.

Furious, she stalked over to the threesome. The men were intent on their conversation and didn't notice her until she barged in between them.

Rhys stared at Lani as she immediately turned her back to him and faced her cousins. pointed a finger at one of the men, whom she called Duke. She spoke to him and the other man in a strange mixture of Pidgin English and other words incomprehensible to Rhys. The men answered her in the same language, one of them looking decidedly sheepish as she continued her harangue. If that's what it was.

Usually, Rhys didn't care for scenes in public, or in private for that matter, but he was thoroughly enjoying this one. His ego should have been offended at Lani feeling she had to defend him from her big bad cousins. Curiously, it didn't bother him at all. He watched in fascination as she grabbed the front of one of the men's shirts and let him have the edge of her tongue.

In a good humor, she had intrigued him. In a temper, she captivated him.

The two men, each a good hundred pounds heavier and at least a foot taller than Lani, only mumbled a few words in defense. One of them held up his hand in a placating gesture, but Lani ignored it. For a full minute more she blasted the men, finally stopping when Rhys put his hand on her arm.

"Lani, take it easy. We were just having a friendly little chat."

Switching to English, she said, "Friendly, my foot. I know why they're here and what they were doing. As you've probably already guessed, these are my cousins, but I won't introduce them." She gave them a look that could peel paint off a wall. "Because you won't see them again. When I'm through with Kimo, he's—"

The taller man said something to her, and the only word Rhys caught that made any sense to him was *Tutu*. He remembered Lani using that name for her grandmother.

Whether it was the reference to her grandmother or something else, Lani's expression changed from fury to one of hard determination. "This has gone far enough," she said to no one in particular. "I'm going to put a stop to it."

Turning abruptly, she walked toward the parking lot beside the bank. Rhys followed. Lani stopped by her car and unlocked it. She placed the box on the backseat, then slammed the back door shut. Her hand was on the latch of the front door when her keys were taken from her.

Whirling around, she saw Rhys standing close to her. "Give me back my keys."

He was unaffected by having her turn her temper on him. "You aren't driving anywhere until you calm down."

She started to tell him what she thought of his interference. Her words disintegrated into a soft sigh when he cupped the back of her neck with one strong hand. Her anger was replaced by another powerful emotion as he looked down at her, the sensual warmth in his eyes holding her enthralled. For a moment she thought he was going to kiss her. Then she was sorry because he didn't.

She didn't give a single thought to the fact that they were standing in the bank parking lot with her co-workers walking by to get to their cars. She could see only Rhys, feel his fingers caressing her sensitive neck, his touch oddly soothing and intimate.

One of the women she worked with honked her horn as she drove by, the sound bringing Lani out of the daze. "I—I need to go talk to my grandmother."

"I'll drive you."

Threads of her temper began to fray. "I'm perfectly capable of driving myself."

"No, you aren't." His fingers encircled her wrist and held her hand out. It was shaking. "It isn't a good idea for someone who is angry to take it out on the roads and other cars."

He was right, which meant she was wrong. She pulled her hand free. "You don't know where you're going. Besides, you're used to driving on the wrong side of the road in England. We'll get killed before we've even gone a block."

He shook his head, amusement glittering in his eyes. "I don't drive on the wrong side of the road. You do. If it makes you feel better, I've driven in the States before and haven't dented a single fender. You either let me drive or I call a cab. You aren't getting behind the wheel while you're upset."

"I'm not upset," she said through clenched teeth. He had no way of knowing her humiliation was as strong as her anger. It wasn't possible for her to explain why she felt as she did. Unless he had been brought up the way she had, he couldn't understand. In the past she had considered her family's attitude amusing. Now she didn't. It had never really mattered before. Now it did.

"Fine," Rhys said. "You're not upset. I'm driving you anyway." A corner of his mouth twitched. "This is your chance to tell me where to go."

He took her arm and led her around the front of the car to the passenger side. With his free hand, he opened the door for her. After he assisted her onto the seat, he carefully shut the door.

Her gaze followed him as he walked back to the driver's side of her car. There was one little thing she should have brought up. If he took her home in her car, it was going to be a bit tricky for him to find his way back to Waikiki. It probably wouldn't make any difference if she pointed that out to him. He was determined to drive her home, and as far as he was concerned, that was that.

Other than telling him which turns to take, Lani didn't make any conversation. She freed her hair from its tight coil, letting the cooling breeze ruffle through it.

When they passed the sign announcing the airport, Rhys had an idea where they were going. It was the same route they had taken before. Between driving with her and the return trip with Kimo, he was becoming quite familiar with this particular highway.

"Would I be correct," he asked, "in assuming

you aren't going to be giving me a tour of the island?"

"You would be correct."

He gave her a quick glance before returning his attention to the road. She was staring straight ahead. Her hands were clenched together in her lap, and the smile he had become accustomed to was absent. He wanted to see it again.

"Would it help if I said your cousins weren't really bothering me?"

"No."

Rhys smiled. She was still seething. It seemed to him she was overreacting to the incident in front of the bank. Her cousins might have made a nuisance of themselves for a short time, but no harm was done. If anyone should be put out, it should be he. Maybe he would have been if he didn't understand how her family must feel about a stranger bothering her. They had no way of knowing that the last thing he wanted to do was hurt her. All he wanted to do was get to know her, spend a little time with her so he could unravel the tangled feelings he felt for her.

"You said the day of the race that Kimo was protective of you. So why are you so angry? I would think you would be used to having your cousins watching over you."

"That doesn't mean I have to like it. When I was a teenager, I didn't mind having my cousins in the background whenever I went out to a dance or to the beach. They intimidated or scared off anyone who was bothering me. At twenty-seven, I don't need their constant guarding any longer. I have to put a stop to it."

"How do you propose to do that?"

"I'm going to talk to my grandmother. One word from her and they'll back off."

Rhys didn't comment. He thought it was doubtful her grandmother would relinquish her strict guardianship just because Lani wanted it. Habits of a lifetime were extremely difficult to break.

When they arrived at her grandmother's house, Lani suggested he remain in the car.

Turning in the seat so he could see her better, he removed his sunglasses and slipped them in a shirt pocket. "I'll come with you."

"I don't think that's such a good idea. If you don't want someone watching your every move during your vacation, you'll let me handle this."

"You fought one battle for me today, Lani. You don't need to fight another on my behalf."

She considered what he had said. He wasn't going to back down, which meant she had to if she wanted to talk to her grandmother. "Then you'd better come with me."

This time they went to the front door, rather than using the back gate. Lani didn't bother to knock but opened the door and went in. Rhys followed her to the rear of the house. Her grandmother was standing at a tall worktable in a back room that had one wall of glass facing the ocean. On the surface were several shallow ceramic containers, a bag of soil, a spool of copper wire, and plants in metal cans. A variety of miniature trees stood on a long bench in front of the glass wall. Emma was in the process of planting another bonsai tree in a clay pot when they entered.

She was wearing a bright lemon yellow muu-muu, her hair piled on top of her head as before. A red hibiscus blossom was in her hair above one ear.

"Hello, Tutu," Lani said.

Emma's smile was broad and warm when she looked up from the table and saw her granddaughter. Then her gaze slid to the man standing behind Lani. She stopped smiling. In a torrent of foreign words, the older woman spoke to Lani, obviously displeased.

"Please speak English, Tutu. Mr. Jones doesn't understand our language."

The older woman gave Rhys a look that spoke volumes. It was obvious she couldn't have cared less if he understood her or not. She did as her granddaughter asked, however. "Why have you brought him here?"

"This is Rhys Jones, Tutu. You know about him. Now I would like you to meet him."

All Rhys received in the way of acknowledgment was a brief nod. "Do you have a good reason for bringing him here?"

"Yes."

Emma glanced from Lani to Rhys, then back again. Cleaning her hands on a towel, she said to Lani, "Show your guest to the lanai. I will bring out some refreshments."

"Thank you, Tutu."

Lani led Rhys to the sliding-glass door leading out to the large patio area. She walked over to a round rattan table and gestured for him to sit down. First, he pulled out one of the chairs for her. Once she was seated, he sat in the chair next to her.

"So far, so good," she said with a faint smile. "She's offering you something to drink instead of shoving you out the door."

"Perhaps I should have you taste my drink. She might be tempted to put something in it."

Lani leaned back in her chair, trying to relax but not succeeding. "At least she's willing to talk. Of course, it could be that she's surprised I'm questioning her authority."

"Why? Haven't you ever confronted your grand-mother before?"

"Not about something like this."

Rhys felt an odd satisfaction. She was standing up to her family because of him.

Her grandmother came out of the house carrying a tray. She set it down on the table, then poured pineapple juice into three glasses and handed them out. Rhys stood up and pulled out a chair for the older woman. She sat down with the dignity inbred in her.

Lani knew her grandmother appreciated Rhys's courteous gesture, just as she knew her grandmother wouldn't acknowledge it. Pushing her glass to one side, she leaned forward and rested her arms on the table.

"Tutu, you know I respect your wishes in most things. I understand why you have taken the action you have, but I'm here to ask you to call off the watchdogs you've set on Mr. Jones. The only reason he wanted to contact me was to give me a gift from Richard McGregor. He was delivering the package as a favor for his partner. Now that he's accomplished that, he's going to have a short vacation here before going on to Australia. It's not fair to him to have someone harassing him while he's on the island."

"I need their eyes to watch," Emma said.

"There is nothing to watch. Mr. Jones is not interested in me, Tutu. He is staying in Hawaii to rest, not to be hassled because of me. We do not treat guests rudely, Tutu. You taught me that. He is a guest to this island and should be treated as such."

Emma directed her dark gaze to Rhys. For the first time she spoke directly to him. "You don't look tired to me. Why do you need to rest?"

Lani didn't give him a chance to answer. "He has worked too hard, too long." She ignored the startled look he gave her and concentrated on her grandmother.

The older woman was studying Rhys thoroughly. "So you stay in Hawaii, then go to Australia. You have the kind of job where you can be gone for long periods of time?"

He could have told her of the fourteen-hour days he had been putting in for as long as he could remember, but he doubted she would be impressed or even care. "It's one of the advantages of having your own business," he said.

Lani's grandmother wasn't satisfied. "Lani is very important to me, Mr. Jones. If she is hurt, I am hurt. I have taken care of her all her life. It's a habit I find hard to break. If I offended you in any way, I will apologize."

He knew that hadn't been easy for her to say, which was why it meant more than it would have otherwise. "There's no need, Mrs. Makena. I understand."

For the first time since they had arrived, Emma smiled. "I appreciate that. I'm pleased to hear you aren't interested in my Lani."

Rhys sipped his juice, then set the glass down on the table. "I didn't say that."

The smile disappeared. "Then what are you saying?"

Lani kicked his shin under the table. She saw him wince, then he jerked his head around to look at her. She ignored him. "He's not saying anything, Tutu. He's a lawyer. They say a lot of things that don't make sense to anyone else."

Rhys made a garbled sound, drawing her gaze back to him. He looked as if he didn't know whether to laugh or strangle her. She saw his mouth open and stood up quickly. She couldn't let him say anything else. He had already said too much.

"I have to drive Mr. Jones back to his hotel," she said, and walked around the table to her grandmother. "Will you tell Kimo and the others that following Mr. Jones is *pau*?" she asked, using the Hawaiian word for "finished."

Emma stared at Rhys thoroughly, as though she were trying to read his mind. "I will think about it."

Lani swallowed her impatience, knowing it wouldn't accomplish anything if she challenged her grandmother any more. She had done all she could do for the moment—with no help from Rhys. She knew her grandmother well. Continuing to argue would only make the older woman more stubborn. Lani also knew what she was going to have to do next. Rather than leave it to her grandmother, she was going to talk to Kimo herself, convincing him to leave Rhys alone and to tell the others to stop.

Bending down, she kissed Emma's cheek. "All right, Tutu. We'll leave you to think about it."

Rhys politely said good-bye and followed Lani back through the house. As they approached her car she held out her hand for her keys. Instead of giving them to her, he took her hand and walked with her to the passenger side of the car. He opened the door, but she refused to get in. "I am quite capable of driving my own car now."

He neither agreed no disagreed as she stood patiently waiting with his hand on the door.

She sighed. "You aren't going to give me my keys, are you?"

"No."

"Any particular reason, since your original one is no longer valid?" She held out her steady hand. "I'm calm, perfectly capable of driving without ending up in a ditch."

"Let's just say I like being in the driver's seat."

His wording made her curious. "In every aspect of your life or just when it comes to cars?"

"We can discuss my aspects over dinner," he said with quiet humor. "Of course, you will have to get in the car first."

Whether they had dinner or drove back to his hotel, Lani knew she was going to have to get into the car. She had learned early she never won when the odds were stacked against her. This was one of those times. She could try some undignified grabbing for the car keys, but that meant searching through his pockets since he wasn't holding them in either hand. She ruled that out as unwise, although it might have been interesting. She got into the car.

He didn't ask her about any restaurants in the area where they might have dinner. In short time she understood why. He knew exactly where he was going. She slowly turned her head to look at him as he parked in her driveway.

"Just so I feel as though I have some say in this," she said, "would you like to have dinner with me?"

"I thought you'd never ask."

Lani smiled. She could become addicted to his dry humor. If she allowed herself to be. Her smile faded. It would be the height of stupidity to become involved with someone who was going to be leaving in a few days. It could also be too late *not* to become involved.

Taking the box with the basket in it from the backseat, she walked to the front door. She paused and turned to Rhys, holding her hand out.

"I need the keys so I can unlock the door."

He obliged by placing the keys in her hand. After the door was unlocked, she opened it and entered the cottage. Heading for her bedroom, she said over her shoulder, "Make yourself at home. I'm going to change."

In her bedroom behind the closed door, she set

the box on her bed and stared at it. All day she
had kept it out of sight under her desk, not wanting to be tempted to open it there. Her co-workers
might ask her questions she'd prefer not to answer. As she looked at the box now she wasn't
sure she wanted to know what was inside. Maybe
Tutu was right. It was better to forget the man.
After all, he had forgotten her. Until now.

Whether it was normal curiosity or a frail wish
for some sort of tie with the man who had fa-
thered her, she tore off the tape holding the box
closed. Folding back the top, she reached in and
sorted through the tissue paper. Her fingers closed
around a piece of wood, and she pulled out the
basket.

As far as baskets went, it wasn't much. The
weaving was loose and uneven. It wouldn't hold
an apple, and a strawberry would fall through
some of the gaps. Afraid it would fall apart, she
set it down on the bed.

Why on earth had Richard McGregor sent her
such a gift? she wondered. If it was supposed to
communicate some message, she couldn't begin
to fathom it. All it told her was that her father
had a peculiar taste in presents.

Irritated because she was disappointed, she
quickly picked up the basket and put it back in
the box. Later she would set it someplace as a
reminder not to expect too much from the past.
She moved the box to her dresser and began to
unbutton her dress.

She felt foolish for expecting something more,
something personal, something more meaningful
than a rather sad basket. Yanking off her belt,
she threw it on the chair. Rhys had said the box
contained a basket, so why had she expected anything different? It was a basket. That was all. Not

a sentimental token of affection, or even an un-sentimental token.

She slipped off her dress and removed the rest of her clothing. She had existed for twenty-seven years without any contact with her father, and she would continue without needing any.

And right now, she had to do something about her guest.

When Lani came out of her bedroom, Rhys was startled to see that all she wore was a large white T-shirt. At least, it was all she appeared to be wearing. The short sleeves had been rolled up several turns, and the hem danced around her bare upper thighs. Everything else but one question left his mind. *Was* the T-shirt the only thing she had on?

The shirt rose as she raised her hands to twist her long hair into a loose coil behind her head. She stuck a pencil-shaped piece of wood through the hair, and he caught a glimpse of black material at the top of her thighs before she lowered her arms.

"I usually take Tommy out for a walk every evening," she said, "Would you like to come along?"

He mentally threw up his hands in surrender. Walking a turtle didn't seem as unusual an occupation as it would have been several days ago.

As they strolled along the beach sand began to fill his leather shoes. He sank down onto the still-warm sand to remove them and his socks, while Lani walked out to the ocean with Tommy in her hand. As he set his shoes and socks aside he looked up, and his breath caught in this throat.

Lani had set Tommy down on the beach. With one swift motion, she lifted the T-shirt up and over her head, then tossed it onto the dry sand. Beneath it she wore two strips of black cloth that adequately but provocatively covered her. The straight line of her spine was interrupted at her shoulder blades by a wisp of material, and another somewhat larger section in a triangular shape clung to her sweetly curving bottom. Every inch of exposed skin was smooth, tanned, and tempting.

After picking Tommy up again, she walked toward the ocean and set the turtle down where the water washed up onto the shore. When he ventured in the direction of the ocean, she turned him around by gently nudging him with her toe. Otherwise she let him wander wherever he wanted to go. Since he wasn't going to set any speed records, he only required an occasional glance to make sure he didn't go too far.

While the turtle trudged along the wet sand, Lani waded into the water. A wave hit her hips, and she swayed but kept her balance. She looked up the beach and saw Rhys was still sitting on the sand. He had slipped on his dark glasses against the glare of the setting sun. She could feel his gaze on her even though she couldn't see his eyes. What was she going to do about him? she asked herself, not really expecting an easy answer.

From an early age she had been taught how to swim safely in the ocean. She had learned to dive through a high wave rather than trying to go over it, how to prevent being pulled under by a strong undertow. She knew not to step on a rockfish and to stay clear of walking on coral in her bare feet.

None of that was helping her deal with the current of attraction dragging her inevitably toward Rhys.

They were oil and water. They had nothing in common except a physical attraction. She knew it would be foolish to become involved with him, but realizing it didn't seem to make any difference. One of her grandmother's earliest warnings that had been drummed into her was to stay away from the tourists. There were to be no exceptions. It was a cardinal rule not to be broken, especially by the members of her family who worked in the Hawaiian shows in Waikiki. The tourists were to be entertained on the stage, not off it. That was all.

Rhys Jones might be considered off limits, but she wanted him. She couldn't understand why something that felt so right could be so wrong. Because desire had never overwhelmed her before, the torrent of sensations she felt whenever she was with him was both frightening and exciting. She might call herself a fool, but she wasn't a coward. She would see this thing through with Rhys—whatever it was.

After making sure Tommy wasn't in any danger, she walked over to her shirt lying on the sand. As quickly as she had stripped it off, she slipped it back on. The material slid over her hips and soaked up some of the moisture off her skin.

Out of the corner of her eye, she saw Tommy slowly edging closer to the water. She walked back and bent down to pick him up. She usually allowed Tommy more time near the water, but this evening they weren't alone.

Walking back up the beach, she stopped several paces away from Rhys. She glanced at his bare feet. "I was wondering if the island would get to you. I'm pleased to see it has."

She was silhouetted against the setting sun as he looked up at her. A faint smile shaped his mouth. "Just because I've taken off my shoes? If that makes you happy, I could remove more."

It was a tantalizing thought. She sank down onto the sand beside him and set the turtle down. "Not in front of the baby. You might shock him."

"Tommy is blind, remember? He wouldn't see a

thing." He looked up from the turtle to her. "Did you have to do that?"

"He's used to the sand. It won't hurt him a bit."

"I meant your shirt."

She frowned. "What about my shirt?"

His gaze slowly slid down to her breasts, where the shirt clung like a second skin to the wet bathing suit underneath. "I was sorry to see you put your shirt back on."

She looked down, confused. She had never felt self-conscious before when wearing a bathing suit. It was a basic article of clothing she had worn all her life. Now she was suddenly aware of her body in a way that had nothing to do with modesty.

Rhys rested his arms on his upraised knees. His body had reacted to the sight of Lani in the brief bikini, and having her near was only making his loins ache even more. Hell, he thought wryly. He had been in a state of semi-arousal since the day he had met her. It would be a miracle if he managed to keep from removing right now her shirt and those two skimpy pieces of material. The tensions tightening his body were also creating a dull ache in the back of his head. Some restful holiday this was turning out to be.

With his gaze on the waves crashing onto the beach, he said casually, "You shouldn't have lied to your grandmother."

Startled, she looked at him. "When did I lie to her?"

"When you told her I wasn't interested in you." Turning to her, he removed his dark glasses as his gaze held hers. "Did you tell her that so she would call off her watchdogs, or because you really believe it?"

Lani picked up a handful of sand and let it run through her fingers. "Both."

His hand closed around hers, forcing her to

stop playing with the sand. "I guess I'll have to change your mind," he said softly.

A current of heat radiated up her arm. Awareness simmered through her, and all he had done was take her hand. She didn't want to think of what would happen to her if he touched her more intimately. Yet it was what she wanted more than breathing.

She tugged to free herself. He refused to release her. He spread her hand palm down over his thigh and covered it with his.

"I've gone past being mildly interested to being strongly attracted," he said. "Even if your grandmother puts every bulky cousin of yours in my way, it won't make any difference."

His thigh was hard and firm. The temptation to stroke that corded strength was potent, and she was unable to relax her hand. "Make any difference about what?"

"About making love to you. It's all I've thought about since I knocked you down."

She ignored the heat that flooded through her at his words. "You can think about it all you want. That doesn't mean it's going to happen."

Lifting her hand to his mouth, he brushed his lips over her warm skin. "Oh, it's going to happen, Lani. It's just a matter of when."

Her breath caught in her throat as he gently sucked on first one finger than another, his tongue stroking her moistened skin. When his teeth nipped the soft flesh of her forefinger, she felt a coil of desire tighten her lower body. She was unaware of the expression of longing entering her eyes as she stared at him.

But Rhys saw her green eyes darken with passion, and triumph slashed through him. The attraction wasn't one-sided. She wanted him.

Suddenly he winced as pain stabbed through

his head. He wanted to shout in frustration. The wretched migraine was back and couldn't have chosen a less opportune moment to return. He let her hand drop and reached into his pocket for his dark glasses, then lowered his head onto his crossed arms resting on his knees.

Obviously it wasn't only tension from work that could bring on one of the damn headaches.

Lani didn't have to ask him what was wrong. She knew. What she didn't know was what to do about it. The last thing he needed at that moment was a bunch of questions. She had to do something, though. She couldn't stand to see him in pain.

She stood and swept up the turtle, then bent down to take his arm. "Let's go back to the cottage. I'll fix us something to eat."

Lani's soft voice penetrated the red haze of pain. This was one of the worst headaches he had ever had, and it had come without a warning. Even getting to his feet was a major ordeal. He accepted her assistance and was glad of the arm she put around his waist as they started across the sand.

Once in the cottage, Lani helped him to her couch. He sank onto the cushions and didn't protest when she gently urged him to lie down. His eyes closed against the shafts of pain splitting his head apart. He opened them when he felt her hand sliding into one of his slacks pockets. Her fingers pressed against him and wiggled as though she was searching for something. When she didn't find what she was looking for, her hand brushed across his waist. He could feel her slight weight as she leaned over to insert her hand into his other pocket.

He closed his eyes again. "I should warn you," he said, his voice husky with pain and the desire that hadn't abated with the onset of the headache, "you might find more than you bargained for if you keep that up."

Her hand stilled for a moment, then she reached further into his pocket. "I'm looking for your pills."

He heard her make a sound of satisfaction when her fingers closed around the small container. He wanted to protest when her weight and hand were removed. A minute later he felt her remove his dark glasses.

Her slender hand went under his head. "Open your mouth, Rhys. I want you to take one of your pain pills."

He obeyed and swallowed when she gave him a drink of water to wash it down. Her hand was removed and a cool cloth was placed over his eyes. When he felt her fingers gently stroking across his forehead, he sighed deeply. Whether from the effects of the pill or her caressing fingers, he slowly slipped into the blessed oblivion of sleep.

Five

The next morning Lani closed her front door silently. Her sandals didn't make a sound as she walked down her porch steps and crossed the grass to the car parked behind hers. Her white suit had narrow black vertical stripes; her blouse was a soft black silk. The wind tugged unsuccessfully at her neatly arranged hair as she slipped in the passenger side of her cousin's car.

Bianca watched as Lani buckled her seat belt. "I did as you asked. I didn't honk the horn or come in like I usually do. Are you going to tell my why I couldn't do either one and why you need a ride to work, or am I supposed to guess?"

Lani's gaze went to her cottage as Bianca backed the car out of the drive. "Rhys Jones is asleep. I didn't want to disturb him."

Bianca kept her attention on the road. "That exhausted, is he?"

Lani gave her cousin a look of irritation. Unfortunately, it didn't have the right effect since Bianca didn't see it. "Sorry to disappoint you, but he had a migraine last night and fell asleep on my couch.

Which is where he still is, so you can put your next question on hold. I didn't sleep with him."

"That explains why you didn't want me to honk my horn or come in but not why you need a ride to work. Is something wrong with your car?"

"I left it for Rhys to use so he can go back to his hotel if he ever wakes up. I was getting worried when I found him still asleep this morning. Either that pain pill he took was strong or the headache wore him out. One of the women I work with gets migraines, and she says the only thing she can do to get over them is to go to bed. They knock her out. Apparently they do the same to Rhys."

"How are you going to get back home? Did you forget I have a class after work on Tuesdays?"

"I haven't thought that far ahead. I'll figure it out later."

Bianca gave her cousin a brief glance, her expression unusually serious. "While you're figuring that out, you'd better give some thought to what you're going to do about Rhys Jones. Tutu called the house last night and asked Kome and Joel to wait for you outside the bank this afternoon. They are supposed to make sure you get home all right. If the *haole* is with you, they are to wait until he's gone again and to make sure he returns to his hotel alone."

Lani swore under her breath. "I asked her to leave him alone."

"She's afraid of lightning striking twice in the same place, doing the same damage," Bianca murmured.

"I'm not my mother and Rhys Jones isn't Richard McGregor. This situation isn't anything like my mother's."

Bianca asked the question Lani had asked herself. "Exactly what is the situation between you and Rhys Jones?"

"Confusing, scary, bewildering, explosive. Pick one. They all fit."

Bianca pursed her lips and whistled, a habit she had when she was surprised. "It sounds uncomfortable."

Lani had to agree with her. Her feelings for Rhys could create a real hazard to her peace of mind. "I don't know what it is. I do know I'm not going to let Tutu stop me from finding out."

When they had to stop at a red light, Bianca looked at her cousin. "I hope you know what you're doing, Lani," she said, concern in her voice. "It isn't wise to cross Tutu. She's against this Rhys Jones, and if you continue to see him, she will make it very difficult for you with the family."

"I wonder if that's why my mother didn't go to England. The whole family has been told the story of how the evil Richard McGregor abandoned his wife and unborn child. You know the tale. You've heard it as long as I have. Always the same version. Always from Tutu's point of view. Have you ever stopped to wonder if there is more to it than Tutu has told us?"

The light turned green but Bianca didn't see it. She was staring at Lani. "Have you gone crazy on me? What has that Englishman been feeding you? Fairy stories?"

"I haven't discussed Richard McGregor with Rhys except for the night I told him who I was. The question I just asked you was one I've asked myself for years. Rhys has nothing to do with it."

The man behind them honked his horn several times, forcing Bianca to pay attention to what she was supposed to be doing.

After a few minutes she asked, "Lani, are you suggesting Tutu lied about what happened to your mother? Look at the evidence. Your father left for England before you were born and never came back. You've never met him because he has ignored your existence until now. Your mother died of a broken heart when you were three years old. Those are the facts."

"The facts according to Tutu. I can't help wondering if she left out something."

"Like what?"

"Like perhaps she insisted my mother stay here instead of leaving the island. All I've ever heard about my mother was how quiet and docile she was. No one has ever had a bad thing to say about her. I've been told she was sweet, delicate, and sensitive. She doesn't sound like the type of person who would be able to stand up to Tutu."

"How long have you been thinking like this?"

Lani shrugged. "About twenty years, give or take a year."

Bianca's head jerked around. "You're kidding!"

The car swerved, and Lani quickly reached across the seat to grab the wheel. "Are you trying to get us killed? Watch where you're going."

Bianca regained control of the car and her surprise. "So what are you going to do now?"

Lani didn't have to ask what her cousin meant. "I've always done basically what Tutu wanted. When she said she didn't want me to go to college on the mainland, I didn't go, even though I wanted to see what California was like. I didn't argue with her when she made the arrangements with Uncle Kale for me to live in his cottage. None of those things mattered enough to me to fight her. Nothing was ever important enough."

"And Rhys Jones is?"

"Yes."

Bianca stopped the car in front of Lani's bank. As her cousin unfastened her seat belt she said seriously, "I hope you know what you're doing."

Lani paused with her hand on the door latch. "So do I."

She got out of the car, waved to her cousin, and walked into the bank.

Everything was as usual. The bank wasn't robbed, the work piled up, and she was as busy as ever. A little after ten, however, she received a phone call that was anything but normal.

It started as any other call. She picked up the receiver and said, "Lani Makena."

A male voice said, "Good morning."

For several seconds Lani didn't speak as the sound of his voice raced over her nerve endings, electrifying them. "Rhys?"

"As far as I know. Since you don't have any coffee, I'm waking up cold turkey."

"How are you feeling?"

"Lonely."

She smiled. "Tommy isn't much of a conversationalist. I was referring to your headache."

"Thanks to your soothing fingers and Dr. Harcourt's prescription, the migraine seems to have disappeared."

"Good. I take it you found my note?"

"I couldn't miss it. It was the first thing I saw when I went into the kitchen since it was sticking out of a plateful of fruit. Your note lacked somewhat in sentiment but was informative. Except for one little thing about my using your car."

"What? You should know the way to your hotel by now."

She could hear the amusement in his voice as he said, "I've never acquired the talent of hot-wiring a car, so it would help if I had the keys."

Her smile broadened. "They're above the visor on the driver's side."

"I trust you didn't lock the car." He didn't give her a chance to reply, but added, sounding grumpy,

"I think I've got cabin fever. I'm not used to having nothing to do."

It hadn't occurred to Lani, or apparently to his doctor, that a workaholic would have difficulty adjusting to not having work to sustain him.

"There are a number of things you can do," she said. "Go for a swim, go shopping, take one of the tours, charter a boat to one of the other islands, learn to scuba-dive."

He didn't comment on any of her ideas. After a short pause all he said was, "I'll be outside the bank at three-thirty."

The line went dead. It was the exact opposite of the way she was feeling. Just hearing his voice had her blood singing. He made her feel more alive than she had ever felt in her life. She didn't understand why it was Rhys who had that effect on her. One thing she did know was she was determined to do whatever she had to, to continue seeing him.

Even if it wouldn't be for long.

She was late leaving the bank due to a last-minute problem. It was a little after four o'clock before she was finally able to put the cover over her computer terminal. The security guard opened the locked door for her and she walked out of the building. It took a moment for her eyes to adjust to the bright sunlight. Shading them with her hand, she looked toward the curb, expecting to see her car. It wasn't there.

She felt a hand at her waist at the same time she heard a familiar British voice speaking in her ear. "I had better luck finding the keys then I did a parking space. We have a little walk ahead of us."

Her heart pounding with delight, she looked up

and saw Rhys smiling down at her. He was wearing his dark glasses and had obviously gone to his hotel room. He was wearing different clothes, a pair of white slacks and a light gray shirt.

He stroked the soft skin under her eyes with his forefinger. "You look tired. Rough day?"

"Just a busy one."

"I thought perhaps it was because you didn't get much sleep last night. At least this time you got the bed and I took the couch. We need to discuss these sleeping arrangements." His finger skimmed over her cheek, then traced the fullness of her bottom lip. His eyes darkened when he felt the tip of her tongue brush his finger. "And soon," he added roughly.

"Rhys, I have to warn you about my family. Before we go any further, you need to know my grandmother hasn't changed her mind. You might have some trouble if you continue to see me."

"I guessed as much. I've had two shadows since I left your house around noon." He brought his other hand up and framed her face between his palms. "Let's give them something to report to your grandmother."

He lowered his head and kissed her. It wasn't possible for her to resist. To deny the pleasure he gave her wasn't in her. His lips were warm and gentle on hers, and she pressed against him wanting more. All too soon, he raised his head, his eyes warm and sensual as he gazed down at her.

His hand returned to her waist, and he kept her locked against his side as they started walking away from the bank. Even though he shortened his stride, Lani had to walk quickly in order to keep up with him.

Bemused by the suddenness of his appearance and by his kiss, she had momentarily forgotten what he had said about having shadows. She was about to turn around to confirm her suspicions, but the pressure of Rhys's hand increased.

"They're there," he said quietly. "They're like an irritating itch I can't scratch."

"I'm sorry. I'd hoped Tutu would call them off. I didn't know until this morning that she hadn't. Bianca gave me a ride to work and told me her brothers were assigned today's guard duty."

Reaching her car, Rhys opened the door for her. "If having two shadows wherever I go is the price I have to pay to see you, I'll gladly pay it."

He shut her door once she was in the car, then slid into the driver's seat. Whether for his own benefit or for the two men watching, he reached for her and pulled her to him. This time he took her mouth with a devastating hunger. Lightning flashed and thunder roared—and the sky was perfectly clear. Needs rose to meet desire as his tongue surged into her mouth. He deftly plucked out the pins holding her hair in its neat coil and combed through the silky strands. Spreading his fingers, he held her head still as he slanted his mouth over hers to deepen the sensual assault.

Lani made a soft sound deep in her throat as his tongue twined with hers. Pleasure held an edge of pain, for she knew this might be all she would have, the heaven she found in his arms. She clung to his shoulders, holding on to what she had. It was magic, an illusion she had to grasp before it disappeared.

Rhys felt his control slipping and grabbed for it, drawing back from Lani even when it was the last thing he wanted to do. Reluctantly, he reached up and clasped her wrists to lower her arms. He gazed into her eyes, seeing a reflection of his desire. Her mouth was moist, her breathing as rapid as his own. Australia, England, his work, everything seemed very far away at that moment. His whole world was centered on the woman next to him.

Pressing her back into her seat, he fastened her seat belt, then his own. He needed the physical restraint since his own wasn't all that strong.

After a moment, when he had himself some-what under control, he turned to her. "We've gone through several phases rather quickly, and we're moving on to another one. You're going to have to decide whether or not you're willing to take that next step, whether you want to go against your family in order to be with me. I'm not talking about casual walks on the beach or a friendly tour of the island. I want you under me in my bed. I want your legs and arms around me, your body hot and slick against mine."

His words sparked flash fires within her, con-juring up pictures that had her heart skipping. Her voice was strangely breathless as she asked, "For how long?"

"The way I feel right now, I'd like to keep you in bed for a week." He paused, knowing what she wanted to hear but unable to say the words. "I'm not going to lie to you and make promises I can't keep. I'm not making any commitments for hap-pily-ever-afters. I doubt if I'll forget you, but I won't say I'll ever be back. I'm exactly what your grandmother thinks I am and what she's afraid of except I won't leave you with a reminder, as Rich-ard McGregor did to your mother."

Something twisted painfully inside her. He cer-tainly didn't sugarcoat his intentions, she thought. "I should hate you." He looked startled and she went on. "Being with you goes against everything I've been taught. You're *kapu*, forbidden, and I want to make love with you until I forget who you are, who I am. Until all that matters is the magic we find in each other."

Rhys's body hardened as her words inflamed him. He reached out to take her hand, but she held it up to ward him off. "No. Don't touch me. I can't think straight when you do and I have to say this." When he lowered his hand, she continued. "I thought I had everything I could possibly want—a good job, a close family, friends. I thought I was happy, that I wasn't missing a thing. There was no reason to change any part of my life. I've never had to oppose my grandmother because I basically wanted the same things she wanted for me."

"What about the rest of the family? This island seems lined with wall-to-wall male cousins."

"They do whatever Tutu wants. Right now she wants to keep me away from you." Lani looked down for a few seconds, then faced him again. "She has made you *kapu*. To go against her wishes will be difficult, since she will do whatever she can to keep us apart. I think I should warn you that it could get unpleasant."

He gave her one of his rare smiles. "It sounds like you've made a decision."

It wasn't fair for him to smile at her like that, she thought helplessly. "I have. You make me feel things I've never felt before, Rhys. I don't expect any promises, nor will I make any. I can't guarantee I can protect you from being harassed by my family, and I can't say I won't have regrets once you leave the island and me." She smiled faintly. "It's not easy to admit I want to disregard everything my family wants for me, and it won't be easy to do it. But some needs are stronger than others."

Rhys was no longer smiling. He was stunned. He had asked for the moon and she had given him the universe. He didn't dare touch her now or he wouldn't be able to stop. He could wait. If he didn't have to wait long.

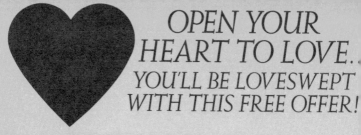

OPEN YOUR HEART TO LOVE...
YOU'LL BE LOVESWEPT WITH THIS FREE OFFER!

HERE'S WHAT YOU GET:

1. FREE! SIX NEW LOVESWEPT NOVELS! You get 6 beautiful stories filled with passion, romance, laughter, and tears...exciting romances to stir the excitement of falling in love... again and again.

2. FREE! A BEAUTIFUL MAKEUP CASE WITH A MIRROR THAT LIGHTS UP!
What could be more useful than a makeup case with a mirror that lights up*? Once you open the tortoise-shell finish case, you have a choice of brushes...for your lips, your eyes, and your blushing cheeks.

*(batteries not included)

3. SAVE! MONEY-SAVING HOME DELIVERY! Join the Loveswept at-home reader service and we'll send you 6 new novels each month. You always get 15 days to preview them before you decide. Each book is yours for only $2.09—a savings of 41¢ per book.

4. BEAT THE CROWDS! You'll always receive your Loveswept books before they are available in bookstores. You'll be the first to thrill to these exciting new stories.

BE LOVESWEPT TODAY — JUST COMPLETE, DETACH AND MAIL YOUR FREE-OFFER CARD.

FREE – LIGHTED MAKEUP CASE!
FREE – 6 LOVESWEPT NOVELS!

- NO OBLIGATION
- NO PURCHASE NECESSARY

(DETACH AND MAIL CARD TODAY.)

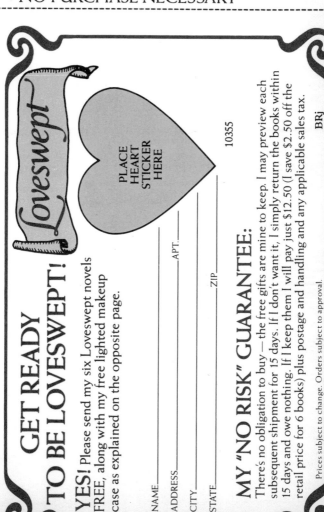

GET READY TO BE LOVESWEPT!

YES! Please send my six Loveswept novels FREE, along with my free lighted makeup case as explained on the opposite page.

NAME _____

ADDRESS _____ APT. ____

CITY _____

STATE _____ ZIP _____

10355

MY "NO RISK" GUARANTEE:

There's no obligation to buy — the free gifts are mine to keep. I may preview each subsequent shipment for 15 days. If I don't want it, I simply return the books within 15 days and owe nothing. If I keep them I will pay just $12.50 (I save $2.50 off the retail price for 6 books) plus postage and handling and any applicable sales tax.

BRj

Prices subject to change. Orders subject to approval.

REMEMBER!

- The free books and gift are mine to keep!
- There is no obligation!
- I may preview each shipment for 15 days!
- I can cancel anytime!

(DETACH AND MAIL CARD TODAY)

POSTAGE WILL BE PAID BY ADDRESSEE

BUSINESS REPLY MAIL
FIRST-CLASS MAIL   PERMIT NO. 2456   HICKSVILLE, N.Y.

Loveswept

Bantam Books
P.O. Box 985
Hicksville, NY 11802-9827

NO POSTAGE
NECESSARY
IF MAILED
IN THE
UNITED STATES

"We'll take it a day at a time and see what happens," he said, touching her hair briefly.

He started the engine and pulled away from the curb. Several feet behind them, another car edged into the traffic. Lani saw almost immediately Rhys wasn't taking the route to her house. He was headed in the opposite direction. He was literally in the driver's seat, and she had an idea where he was going. After those arousing kisses and their conversation, she expected him to take her to his room. Anxiety flooded through her, yet it was immediately swept away by undeniable desire and a sense of rightness she'd never felt before.

Rhys parked at the Outrigger Hotel, but didn't take her inside. Instead, he held her hand and led her across the street to the International Market Place, a popular tourist attraction amidst banyan and coconut trees.

As they made their way through the crowds of people Rhys released her hand and slipped his arm around her waist, holding her close to his side.

"What are we doing here?" she asked.

"I'm hungry. I thought we would get something to eat."

There were a number of different places where they could sample a variety of foods, but Rhys wasn't interested in any of them. His destination was the restaurant called Trader Vic's, the place where Kimo worked.

After they were seated at a table near the stage, as Rhys had requested, Lani leaned forward in her chair. "Kimo is right. You are one *pupule haole*."

"What's *pupule*?"

"Crazy. Bianca's brothers, Kome and Joel, just came in and are taking a table by the door. We can't leave without passing them. Kimo will be on the stage in about twenty minutes. You're in the middle like the filling of a sandwich about to be mashed by two thick slices of bread."

Rhys chuckled. "I've never thought of myself as a sandwich before."

Suddenly he frowned as he realized she was too far away. He pushed her skirt aside so he could grip the chair and pull it over beside his. He wasn't satisfied until her leg was pressed against his. Then, under the cover of the table, he laid his hand on her firm thigh.

"You are *pupule*," she said breathlessly.

He smiled. "What's so crazy about wanting to touch a beautiful woman's body?"

She sighed. "Apparently I'm not exactly in my right mind either since I'm not doing a thing to stop you."

When the waiter approached their table with menus, she was relieved to see he was someone she didn't know. Without consulting Rhys as to what he might like, she ordered their drinks. "I'll have a fizz, and bring a pineapple cocktail for the gentleman."

Nodding, the waiter left their table. Rhys ignored the menu in front of him. "I've been ordering my own drinks for quite a few years now, Lani."

"And I'm familiar with the drinks here. You aren't supposed to drink anything alcoholic, so I ordered you fresh pineapple juice on the rocks."

He leaned back in his chair, although he didn't remove his hand from her thigh. "My mother's in Australia. I don't need another one."

She studied him for a several moments, trying to determine if he was angry or not. "I won't apologize for wanting to make things easier by interpreting the drinks menu for you." She reached under the table and twined her fingers with his, then brought their clasped hands up and rested them on the table. "You like to be in control, don't you, Rhys? That's why you don't like my ordering drinks for you. That's why you hate having those headaches. They forced you to take a vacation you didn't want. They temporarily take control, and there isn't anything you can do about it."

He missed the feel of her slender thigh under his hand. "How clever of you to have figured everything out about me in such a short time. It took the doctor several weeks of tests before he made a diagnosis."

She overlooked his sarcasm. "Why do you feel you have to work yourself into the ground, Rhys? Why did you have to be forced to take time off?"

He surprised them both by giving her an honest answer. "The easiest explanation is that I like my work and there isn't anything I prefer more that could take its place. The more complicated answer is I didn't like being poor."

Lani remembered he'd said waiting tables was only one of the jobs he'd had when he was getting an education. He had also told her his father had died when he was young and his mother had a tea shop. Because of circumstances, Rhys had had to work for everything he had. Work had become the solution, and the solution had become a way of life. Now his body was protesting against the constant diet of work by giving him migraines. If he kept it up, he could work his way to ulcers, to be followed by a heart attack.

Their drinks arrived, and the waiter asked if they wanted to order dinner. Rhys said he'd prefer to wait. The waiter nodded and left. Rhys and Lani lifted their drinks in a silent toast to each other. They had only taken a sip when drums began to beat and the lights on the stage changed. The floor show had begun. During the next hour it was impossible to hold a conversation. Lani had seen the show or ones like it many times, but Rhys hadn't. The extravagant costumes and the songs and dances were full of the spirit of the islands, and were geared for the tourists who wanted a more flamboyant style of entertainment.

Lani noticed Rhys was particularly attentive to the female Tahitian dancers with their elaborate plume headresses and gyrating hips. He also watched the dances of the different islands—Fiji, Samoa, and New Zealand—but not with the same enthusiasm. She smiled at his startled reaction when warriors raced on stage, jumping, stomping, and swirling long knives. At last all but one of the dancers left the stage, leaving the solo warrior swirling a baton lighted at each end, the flames glowing on the darkened stage.

"We should leave now," Lani said, leaning over to speak to Rhys. "Kimo is on next."

Rhys looked at her in surprise. "I'd like to see what he does. I've never seen a mountain sing or dance before."

She shook her head. "You're going to have to trust me. You don't want to stay. When the torch dancer is through, a single dancer will come to the front of the stage under a spotlight. While she dances, the stage will go completely dark for a few minutes to enable the stagehands to change the backdrop for Kimo's performance. That's when we'll leave."

Everything happened exactly as she said. The stage went dark and a dancer appeared in the spotlight. She was dressed in a brief lavalava—a rectangular piece of material wrapped low around her hips—with a bikini top and a flower lei to complete her outfit. As several guitars played a soft, rhythmic melody she began to dance, her hips undulating.

Lani grabbed Rhys's hand and led him around the tables between theirs and the exit. It was probably a vain hope, but she wanted to get out of the dining room without Kome and Joel seeing them.

Rhys tightened his hold on Lani's hand as they left the restaurant. "Are you going to tell me why we couldn't have stayed to see Kimo's act?"

"During the finale the performers come out into the audience and pick people to go up on stage and dance. Kome and Joel would have sent a message back to Kimo, telling him we were there. He would have made sure one of the girls came to our table and dragged you on stage."

Rhys started to laugh until he saw there was no humor in Lani's eyes or voice. "Would that have been so bad? It's all in good fun, isn't it?"

"Usually. It's hard telling what Kimo might do once you're up on the stage. I didn't want to take the chance he might try to embarrass you. It's something he could do very easily, and there wouldn't be anything you could do about it."

They had reached the entrance of the International Market Place. Rhys drew her out of the way of the other people entering and leaving. His expression was a mixture of anger and irritation as he looked down at her.

"I can't remember ever being protected as much as I have these last few days." He placed his fingers under her chin, lifting her head so he could see her face. "Why are you doing it?"

"I feel responsible."

He was astounded, his eyes widening with shock. "For me?"

"For whatever happens to you while you're on the island," she clarified. She pointed in the direction of his hotel across the street. "If you had any sense, you would go to your room, pack your bags, call the airport, and fly immediately to Australia or back to England. It would save both of us a lot of trouble."

He shook his head. "I was in trouble the first time I kissed you. If I had any sense, I wouldn't keep kissing you. Or want to do more than kiss you." He pulled back, needing some distance between them. "We still haven't had dinner. Is there anyplace we can go where we won't run into one of your cousins, or is that impossible?"

She knew just the place. They returned to her car, and she told him to take the road to Makaha. Before they reached her house, however, she gave him directions to a small restaurant on a side road. It wasn't fancy. In fact from the outside, the building looked as if it would fall over in a strong wind. The paint on the long sign over the porch was faded and unreadable. Inside were simple picnic tables with heavy plastic tablecloths tacked to them.

And they served the best food Rhys had ever eaten.

It wasn't until they were eating squares of a coconut pudding Lani called haupia that it occurred to Rhys he hadn't had even a hint of a headache all day. It certainly wasn't because he was relaxed—at least not completely. His desire for Lani Makena was becoming a constant ache, a different type of pain than he had been suffering from with the migraines.

Lani glanced up from her plate of haupia and saw a pained expression in his eyes. "What's wrong?" she asked quickly. "Is your headache back?" She started to stand. "We can leave right now."

He grabbed her hand, keeping her in her chair. "It isn't my head. I'm having a problem with a different part of my anatomy that has nothing to do with migraines."

Her breath caught in her throat. The very air began to crackle with tension. The attraction between them tightened to an almost unbearable degree as she met his heated gaze.

Rhys picked up one of the small squares of haupia and offered it to her. Leaning forward, she bit off a small piece, her eyes held by his. He drew back, and her tongue swept across her lips. His gaze lowered to her mouth. Dropping the haupia on his plate, he reached over and pressed his finger to her lips. Her tongue brushed his finger, her teeth nipped lightly.

He withdrew his hand, his gaze still holding hers as he removed some cash from his wallet.

"Are you ready?" he asked, throwing the money on the table.

Lani wondered if he meant, was she ready to leave the restaurant or ready for something else. In either case, she was.

After they left the restaurant, there was no discussion where they would go next. It wasn't necessary. A decision had been made, even though neither had spoken aloud.

Rhys parked the car in the driveway of her cottage and pocketed the keys as he came around to open her door. He extended his hand to her, and she placed hers in it, surrendering more than her hand.

It wasn't a time to talk of choices. There wasn't one any longer.

Six

Rhys drew her out of the car and into his arms. There was nothing tentative or teasing about his kiss. He took her mouth with blatant male hunger, and she responded with her own brand of passion. She was swept up into his arms as he turned away from the car. Her arms encircled his neck and her breasts were crushed against his chest as his mouth demanded more from her.

The first indication she had that they weren't going to the cottage was when she felt the wind off the ocean tousling her hair. Yet she knew it would take more than the fresh salty air to cool the molten heat flowing through her veins. She didn't ask what his intentions were. She understood.

Rhys slowly lowered her feet to the sand, watching her eyes as her lower body came into contact with his hard arousal. As she slid down his body her skirt bunched up between them. He clenched the material covering her bottom, gathering it in his hands. Only a brief piece of silk separated his hands from her warm bare flesh.

His lips grazed her soft throat. Her exotic scent

and taste blended with the sultry night and the sounds of the waves crashing onto the shore. He couldn't explain why he had brought her to the beach, instead of to the relative comfort of her bedroom. She was a child of the islands, a woman of paradise. The elements of nature suited her more than the enclosed walls of her cottage.

He slipped her jacket off, and his knuckles brushed her skin as he peeled off her shirt. Quickly, he unfastened her skirt and skimmed it over her hips. Bringing his gaze slowly up, Rhys felt his heart slam in his chest. She stood in front of him wearing a delicate lace-trimmed teddy the color of Devon cream. It clung to the mounds of her breasts, the satiny material clearly emphasizing their shape. He could only look at her, allowing his gaze alone to touch her until he got himself under control.

When he at last raised his hands to cup her breasts, he realized the fantasies he'd had of touching her didn't come close to reality. Her flesh under the smooth cool fabric was hot, the contrast jolting him. He shuddered as she lifted her hands and began to unbutton his shirt.

"I want to touch you, all of you," she said softly, bringing her lips to his bared chest.

The strong ocean breeze did nothing to dampen his desire. Each taste, each touch heightened his pleasure and fed his hunger. Taking the hint of her hands tugging at his shirt, he shrugged out of it and let it drift down onto the sand. Male satisfaction and pride flowed through him as he caught the expression of approval and desire in her eyes as her gaze roamed over him.

Lani stood still as he slowly lowered the thin straps of her teddy down her arms. It slid over her breasts to her waist, and she shivered. Moving her hips as she did when she danced the hula, she kept her gaze on him as the teddy fell to the sand.

The sight of her naked body against the backdrop of the pounding ocean, with the wind tossing her hair around her face and over her bare shoulders, snapped his control. He was going to be burned alive when he made her his. And he couldn't wait any longer.

His hands shook as he pulled her into his arms, crushing her soft naked length to his hard throbbing body. He covered her moist lips with devastating hunger, his hands caressing and worshipping wherever they touched and gripped.

Of all the emotions coursing through him, he had to reach for gentleness, hoping for a little as he lowered her to his shirt on the sand. It had been so long. No, he corrected himself. It had been forever since he had wanted a woman as he craved Lani. Her hair spread out in glorious disarray, her eyes never leaving him as he quickly kicked off his shoes and stripped off the rest of his clothes.

He came down beside her and pulled her against him. Pleasure flared within her, and she feared its fire would consume her before he at last made love to her. He pressed his knee between her legs, and her blood ran hotter than the lava flowing from the volcano on the Big Island. Before, passion had simply been a word she used for a flower or a perfume, never to describe her feelings.

They moved together as though they had known each other intimately before, naked bodies pressed close, hands and mouths voraciously seeking. Yet there were surprises in every caress, every stroke. Each was greedy to take, yet generous to give.

Beneath the desire was a tenderness Rhys hadn't expected. That tenderness had him swallowing with difficulty when Lani raised her arms in invitation.

"Are you sure, Lani? There's no going back after you become mine."

Her arms encircled him, her hands pressing against his back to bring him down to her. "I'm sure. I've never been more sure of anything in my life. I want you to make love to me."

He came to her then because he could do nothing else. He felt her shudder beneath him as he parted her legs and slipped between them. Holding her shoulders, he gently eased into her, and the world shattered around him.

Lani murmured his name once as he thrust within her. Then she couldn't make a sound as she fell into the well of passion. She was one with him, moving with him in a dance more beautiful than anything she had ever known. All the splendor of the islands was nothing compared to the pleasure they found together, and they cried out wordlessly, clinging to each other, as they were hurled into the flames waiting for them.

The waves continued to collapse on the sandy shore as they slowly recovered from the tumultuous delight. The thick palm leaves crackled as the wind tossed them. Paradise existed as before around them, and now in them.

Rhys held her close as he attempted to put a name to the feelings rushing through him. There was only one word that kept appearing in his mind. Love. Stunned, he rolled onto his back, carrying her with him. He was actually in love with her.

Lani felt the sudden tension in his body and wondered what was wrong. How could anything be wrong after such wondrous lovemaking? It took an enormous effort, but she managed to raise her head and look down at him. Even in the dark, she could see and sense the strain in his eyes and body. Either his headache had come back . . . or he was regretting what had just happened.

"What's wrong?" she asked quietly.

The incessant wind brushed her hair over his chest. He wrapped one long curl around his finger. "Nothing's wrong. It takes a little getting used to, that's all."

"What takes getting used to?"

"When I get used to it, I'll let you know."

She made a sound of surprise as she was suddenly lifted away from him, then up into his arms. He carried her to the ocean, not releasing her until the waves swelled around his hips. Lowering her so she was standing in front of him, he held her tightly and took her mouth with a hunger unabated by their lovemaking.

Waves buffeted them with the power of nature as a primitive surge of the senses renewed itself. Clinging to him with her arms around his neck, Lani felt his hands slide over her bottom to her thighs. Her legs were lifted and wrapped around his hips, and she gasped as he slid into her.

When Lani let herself out of her cottage the following morning, there was no car waiting for her and Rhys wasn't sleeping on the couch. During the night, they had showered off the sand and salt water and, exhausted, had collapsed on her bed.

Habit had her waking at her usual time without the benefit of an alarm clock. Though reluctant to leave her bed and Rhys's warm body, she dressed quietly and quickly while he slept. This time she hadn't phoned Bianca to beg a ride to work. She took her own car, making one stop along the way to Honolulu. Rhys might not appreciate her making plans for his day, but she would deal with his anger later. She had the impression he was a man who didn't know how to relax, or possibly even felt guilty doing anything but work. Inactivity was grating against his nature, so she had arranged for something for him to do.

Whether it was what he wanted was something else again.

When Lani returned home that afternoon, she tore off the scarf holding her hair back as she got out of her car. Shaking her head to loosen the thick curls, she walked up the porch steps, wondering how Rhys had enjoyed his day.

The door wasn't locked, which meant he'd either forgotten to lock it when he left or was there. It didn't take long for her to discover the cottage was empty—except for the sea horses and the turtle.

In only a few minutes she changed out of her dress into her bikini. Since she didn't have any idea when and if Rhys would be coming back, she was going to go about her day as usual. With a towel looped around her neck, she picked up the turtle and took him down to the beach. After giving him sufficient time to wander in the wet sand, she made a small corral out of rocks and coconuts and placed Tommy inside where he would be safe. Then she dropped her towel beside him and ran into the ocean, diving through a large wave. Strong strokes took her out past the cresting waves.

The stress of the day dissolved as she skimmed through the water. She had been swimming in the ocean as long as she could remember. Even before she knew how to walk, she had been carried into the water. Over the years she had learned how to respect the sea and the dangers that could be found in its depths. She couldn't imagine living anywhere that didn't have access to the ocean.

Finally, she chose a wave and rode it into the shore. Finding the bottom with her feet, she stood up in hip-deep water and waded the rest of the way in.

Waiting for her with her towel in his hand was Rhys.

At least she thought it was Rhys. She stopped three feet away and stared. The blue eyes, the sandy blond hair, and the wry smile were familiar. The rest wasn't. In place of the immaculate slacks and crisp shirt he usually wore, were a pair of cutoff jeans hung low on his hips and a red aloha shirt with bright blue and yellow hibiscus flowers all over it. He was barefoot, and unless she was very much mistaken, he had a first-class sunburn.

"Rhys?"

He held up the towel. "Have you forgotten me so soon?"

She moved forward and he enclosed her in his arms, wrapping the towel around her. It would be easier to forget her own name, she thought, loving the feel of his body against hers. It had been a long day without him.

"I haven't forgotten you," she murmured. Drying herself off, she stepped back, her gaze going up and down his long frame. "I said your name because I couldn't think of anything else to say until I find out if you're angry or not."

"Now why should I be angry?" He took the towel out of her hands and made her turn around so her back was to him. With gentle care, he dried her hair for her.

"I also wasn't sure it was you," she teased. "You look like a local instead of a tourist."

"Since you were responsible for Aku coming to the cottage this morning, you shouldn't be so surprised I look like this. The man is part fish and tried to turn me into one."

She choked back a laugh. "Do you know what Aku means?"

"The man said barely two words all day. Neither one of them described his name."

"*Aku* means 'tuna.'" Beginning to feel like a spinning top, she let him turn her around again. "Did you enjoy your day?"

"After the initial shock of learning the man's conversation consisted of pointing and grunting, I had a great time. He didn't have to speak. To my amazement, I understood his gestures. Even his silence spoke volumes." Rhys lifted his hand and trailed a single finger down her cheek. "It accomplished what you wanted. I didn't think about work once, and there was no sign of an impending migraine all day. That is why you sent Aku over here, isn't it?"

"That was the general idea."

"I thought I was *kapu*. He introduced himself as your uncle. Why isn't he staying the hell away from me, too?"

"He's Tutu's brother, but he's always done as he pleased, not what she wants him to do. When I phoned him this morning, I told him about you and that you needed some rest and relaxation Hawaiian-style. When Aku said he was going fishing, I asked if he would take you with him."

She didn't add that the main reason she had phoned Aku was because she didn't have to worry about any interference from Kimo or her other cousins if Rhys was with him. None of them would dare cross Aku by following Rhys when he was with the older man. Rhys didn't consider her cousins any sort of threat, but she did.

"I wouldn't call what we did fishing," Rhys said as he followed her over to where she'd left Tommy.

Lani picked up the turtle and brushed off some of the sand clinging to him. She smiled over her shoulder at Rhys. "Did you bring any fish back?"

"Yes."

"Then it sounds to me like you went fishing."

"Aku's method of fishing is like none I've ever seen before. I'm accustomed to using silly things like fishing poles and hooks with bait on them."

Holding Tommy close to her chest, she said hesitantly, "I was hoping you would enjoy diving and spearing fish. You still haven't said whether you did or not."

It occurred to Rhys that she was nervous. He found it endearing, yet at the same time was tempted to let her wonder a little longer. Initially, he hadn't been amused to discover she had made plans for him without consulting him. He had changed his mind, though, as the day became an adventure unlike anything he had ever imagined.

He put his arm around her slender waist and walked beside her toward the cottage. "I can honestly say it was an experience I will always remember. So are these clothes. Once we were on his boat, Aku fumbled around in a locker and tossed these togs at me. I took the hint. The cutoffs ended up being my bathing suit."

Rhys opened the door and urged her into the house ahead of him. He directed her to Tommy's aquarium, and she set the turtle in it. She would have moved away, but Rhys suddenly scooped her up in his arms.

"What are you doing?" she gasped.

Against her lips, he murmured, "I'm saying hello. I don't think I've said it yet."

Her arms slid up around his neck. "Hello," she said, her voice soft and intimate.

As he walked out of the kitchen toward her bedroom he said, "While I was getting my knee scraped on coral and my back sunburned, I thought of what I would do to you when and if I ever got back to you in one piece." His smile was wonderfully sensual. "Now I'm going to carry out each and every one of those thoughts."

A shiver of anticipation ran over her skin. "What about your sunburn? You really should take a shower and rinse off with vinegar. It will help take the heat out of it."

He stopped in the middle of the hall and stared down at her. "When I make love to you, I would prefer not to smell like a salad." Continuing down the hall, he added, "Besides, I'd need more than vinegar to take the heat out of making love to you."

Her heart raced, the drumming of her blood loud in her ears as she saw the desire in his eyes. Even when her feet touched the floor, she felt as though she were floating as he took her mouth with sweet hunger.

Her wet bikini was skimmed off, and she fumbled with the buttons on his shirt, making a frustrated sound when her shaking fingers couldn't accomplish the task.

"It's all right," he said soothingly. "I'll take care of it. I'll take care of everything."

She sighed his name as she leaned into him, oddly helpless as desire made her a willing partner in the race toward the pleasure waiting for them. He caught her up and laid her on her bed, following her down after stripping off his clothes.

Unable to resist the scent of her, the softness of her, yet her compelling strength as she arched under him, Rhys deliberately spread her legs and rested his body on top of hers.

Air had to be dragged into his lungs before he

could even utter her name. "Lani, look at me. I want to see your eyes when I come into you."

Slowly, she raised her long lashes. Even when she felt him fill the aching emptiness within her, she didn't look away. The expression in his eyes, the warmth, the need she saw in them, was almost as intimate as her body taking him deep inside her.

Even though they had burned in the fires of their first passionate joining, this time was twice as hot as Pele's fire.

When Lani had thrown Rhys and Aku together, she'd had no idea Rhys would want to fish again with the elderly Hawaiian. In the next two days, Rhys's sunburn turned into a golden tan and the sun bleached white-blond streaks into his hair. His choice of clothing became markedly different, too, as he returned to her cottage each evening wearing cutoffs and an aloha shirt or T-shirt.

Lani felt like a spectator at an astounding metamorphosis. Except when he took her in his arms. Then she was a participant, an active, willing, loving participant.

She no longer asked Rhys when he was leaving for Australia. It was a question she didn't want answered. Each day was like Christmas, full of excitement, anticipation, and the gift of loving Rhys.

When she returned from work on Wednesday, she thought she saw Kome's Jeep parked alongside the road leading to her cottage. Since whoever it was had his head turned away, she couldn't see if it was her cousin or not. When she arrived home, she phoned Bianca and asked her if Tutu was still requesting that Kome watch Rhys. Her aunt answered the phone and told her Bianca wasn't home. When Lani asked if Kome was there, her aunt was enigmatic, telling her what she wanted to know without actually saying a thing.

As the weekend approached, Lani was feeling the pressure of waiting for something to happen. Soon Rhys would leave, taking her heart with him. She needed to make sure that when he left, he wouldn't have been harmed in any way. She didn't want him to meet the same fate as the sailor who had persistently bothered one of her female cousins. The man had been badly beaten.

She assumed Emma knew by now that Rhys spent almost all his time at her cottage when he wasn't with Aku. Lani didn't like hurting her grandmother by having an affair with Rhys, but she had to grab for the happiness she found with him while it was being offered.

As soon as she arrived home from work on Thursday, she changed clothes, slipping on a pair of white shorts and a mint green cotton sweater. She went into the kitchen to pack a wicker picnic hamper with food. That morning Rhys had suggested they go out to dinner, but Lani didn't want to go to a public restaurant. If they were being watched, she wanted to go somewhere where they wouldn't be followed. The trick was getting away from the cottage without being seen, and without letting Rhys know she was trying to evade her cousins.

She heard the front door open and close, signaling Rhys's return. He called her name and she raised her voice to answer. "I'm in the kitchen."

She continued washing the fruit, not at all surprised that her pulse had begun to race. He had only to say her name or be in the same house, and her senses were heightened.

A hand snaked around her waist and pulled her

up against a hard male body. He whirled her around, then soundly kissed her.

When he raised his head, he smiled down at her. "Hello, *ipo*."

She stared at him. He had just called her darling in Hawaiian. "Has Aku been giving you Hawaiian lessons?"

"He manages to work a word in now and then."

"*Ipo* is a rather strange word for him to be teaching you while you're fishing."

"You'd be surprised what we talk about." Reaching into the pocket of his cutoffs, he held up an object. "Look what I found on the beach where Aku keeps his outrigger canoe."

He showed her a seashell he had found on the beach, presenting it to her as though it were a rare gem. "Aku said he could show me where the live ones are in the coral beds. He said they get much bigger than this."

She smiled at the enthusiasm in his voice. "It's a textile cone. I hope Aku also told you that if you pick one up that's alive, you should grab the larger end. It has a venom that can be dangerous if it's small harpoon touches you. Besides, if you want to keep the shell, you have to kill the animal inside."

He hadn't thought about that. Frowning, he murmured, "I'll leave them where they are."

"Good. I was hoping you would say that. Shell collectors freeze them as a humane way of killing the animal inside, but I still prefer to have them remain in the ocean."

He crossed the room and placed the shell on the windowsill. Glancing at the assortment of vegetables, meat, and long slender sticks beside the sink, he asked, "What are you making?"

"I'm putting teriyaki steak strips on those little

sticks." She grinned at him. "You're going to cook them over an open fire on the beach."

"I don't remember volunteering to do any cooking."

She laughed. "You didn't. I just had that terrific idea as I was driving home from work."

He gave her a doubtful look and took a package of lunch meat and some cheese out of the refrigerator. "Just in case my cooking ends up in the sand."

As he placed the small packages into the hamper, he examined the plates and silverware strapped onto the lid. "Very nice. What happened to the basket your father sent you? Did you ever open the box?"

"The basket's in the living room on the floor next to the fish tank. Why?"

He put two apples into the hamper. "Just curious."

"Why are you suddenly curious after all this time?"

He smiled, his eyes glittering with amusement. "An attractive *hapa haole wahine* has been keeping me busy."

She made a choking sound of laughter and surprise. "Aku's lessons seem to be covering a lot. Do you know what *hapa haole wahine* means?"

He looked mildly offended. "Of course. Half-foreign woman."

"Actually it means half-Caucasian. Somehow Hawaiian words sound different with an English accent," she added dryly.

"That's what Aku said," he murmured as he left the kitchen. Actually, Aku hadn't said a thing. He'd just laughed until Rhys was afraid the elderly fisherman would fall out of the canoe.

The basket was in the living room where Lani had said it was. He picked it up and carried it over to the window. It was crudely made with

willow and oak splints. The weaving was crude,
the handle thick and twisted. It was a sorry excuse for a basket, and a poor present for a long-
lost father to give to his daughter.

As far as Rhys was concerned, the basket was
one of the most important objects he had ever
seen in his life. Because of this pathetic basket,
he had met Lani.

Added to Rhys's growing list of firsts was having a picnic on the beach. The sun was low in the
sky, the colors brilliant as Lani spread out a rattan mat on the sand in a place the locals called
Shark's Cove. Because the name accurately described the hazards in that particular area of water, they didn't go for a swim. It was also why
Lani had chosen the cove. None of her family ever
came there, or would think she would go there
either.

She watched Rhys cook over the fire he had
made in a pit surrounded by rocks. He managed
very well, considering it was the first time he had
ever cooked a meal over an open fire. They ate
fruit, fresh vegetables, and all of the teriyaki strips.
She had stopped on the way home from work and
purchased a bottle of wine, and they drank that
while they watched the sun set.

It wasn't until after they had eaten that Rhys
mentioned the odd route she had taken to get to
the beach. "I realize I'm no expert on the high-
ways and byways of this island, but I can tell
when we drive ten miles out of our way. We drove
inland away from the beach only to turn around
and head back. I was puzzled by the sudden turn
into a cane field, too. Would you like to explain
why you did that?"

Lani took a sip of wine, more to stall for time

than because she was thirsty. She came up with a weak explanation. "I thought you might like to see something of the island away from the water."

She looked at him, waiting for him to press the issue, but he didn't. Sprawled out on the mat, he was totally relaxed in tan slacks and a white shirt. As far as she knew, he hadn't had a migraine since last Monday, so his vacation was accomplishing what it was supposed to do. The island had worked its magic.

He glanced up and caught the expression on her face. "You look sad. What are you thinking about?"

She drew her legs up and crossed her arms over them. "I was thinking it will soon be time for you to leave."

He looked out at the ocean and didn't reply for several minutes. "I thought we had gone past your trying to get rid of me."

"That isn't what I meant, Rhys. I'm being realistic. You have your work and your life away from here. Eventually you'll leave. I knew that from the first. I've accepted it."

He sat up abruptly and grabbed her arms, tugging on her until she was kneeling in front of him. "I haven't. The thought of leaving you is something I haven't been able to think about. I don't want to think about it."

She placed her hands on his shoulders. "You have to think about it, Rhys. I've lived here all my life, and I know what this island can do. People get off the plane and are immersed in exotic flowers and a turquoise ocean. They leave their cares and worries behind them as they douse themselves with suntan oil and soak up the atmosphere of paradise. Each comes for a different reason, and most of them find what they wanted. Some tourists want the sea and sand; others a badly needed break from reality. Then there's shopping, Hawaiian history and arts and crafts, perhaps a romantic honeymoon. Real life is put on hold temporarily. It's all very exciting, different, and . . ." She paused, then added with emphasis, "Unrealistic."

"Are you saying what we have is a fantasy?" His fingers tightened on her arms almost painfully. "Because if you are, you're the one being unrealistic."

"It doesn't matter what we call it. A fantasy or unrealistic or an affair. Whatever it is, it's temporary."

She started to pull away, but he wouldn't let her go. His hands moved up to frame her face. "Lani," he began, not sure what he was going to say. "I know we have a few things to work out."

"Like us living in two different countries half a world apart," she said bluntly. "Even the magic of the islands can't do anything for that particular problem."

"I'm working on it."

She wasn't able to ask what he meant. His mouth came down hard on hers, fury and frustration throbbing through him as he lowered her to the mat. His hands swept over her as if to confirm she was there with him. Because it was a public beach, he had to settle for kissing her when all he wanted to do was sink into her, to affirm their being together.

Reluctantly, he raised his head. He saw confusion mixed with desire in her green eyes. Brushing the back of his finger over her cheek, he said quietly, "I want us to be together, Lani. There's a way. We just have to find it."

It seemed an insurmountable problem to her, like trying to build a snowman at the base of a volcano. "Maybe that's what happened between my mother and father," she said sadly. "The differences were too great. Their backgrounds, their cultures, their customs. It's obvious they couldn't work it out."

"But we will." He pushed himself off her, then brought her up to a sitting position, holding her directly in front of him. "Our situation isn't the same as the one your parents were in, Lani. We aren't the same people. Don't let your grandmother influence you into thinking we don't have a chance."

"You can't deny there are similarities, Rhys."

"Only in nationalities."

She reached out to touch his face because she needed to. "I'm not trying to push for a commitment from you, Rhys. I knew you would be leaving, and I got involved with you anyway." Her smile was ragged around the edges. "I guess what's bothering me is I don't know how long we have before you leave. We haven't had much time to get to know each other."

He released her and sat back on his heels. He had been living a day at a time without thinking past the next opportunity to be with her. Her description of how people reacted to the island fit him as well. The laid-back atmosphere was having an odd effect on him. Since he had become involved with her, he had been drifting along in a haze, so wrapped up in Lani, he had happily let the rest of the world go by. His priorities were changing. Realizing that his work didn't seem as important as it had before stunned him.

When he didn't say anything, Lani turned away. To hide her disappointment that he wasn't contradicting her, she began gathering up the remains of their picnic.

His fingers closed around her wrist. "Lani, stop."

She froze at his touch, cursing herself for starting this. She had pushed, and he had resisted.

There was nothing more to say, yet apparently he thought there was. Now she wasn't sure she wanted to hear it.

Taking a deep breath, she raised her head and met his serious gaze. "I've broken the rules, haven't I?" she said, smiling weakly. "It's probably because I've never played this particular game before. Just forget everything I said."

Her about-face obviously perplexed him. "I can't do that."

"Well, try. This is embarrassing enough."

He stroked her cheek. "For someone who makes his living communicating and settling disputes, I'm not handling this very well. We need more time to work this out. Why don't you come with me to Australia? You can stay with my sister while I take care of my business there, then we can—" He stopped abruptly when he saw the shocked look on her face. "What's the matter?"

"Your *sister*?"

"Yes. She's one of the reasons I'm going to Australia." He shook his head as she continued to stare at him, anger overriding the shock in her eyes. "Why are you looking at me that way?"

"You never told me you had a sister, much less that she was in Australia."

"Does it make all that much difference? She didn't have anything to do with us."

Lani felt sick. He didn't think his having a sister was any of her business. He had only brought her up now to convince her to go to Australia with him. If she'd needed anything else to point out the differences between them, she had it.

Suddenly she heard someone calling her name. She turned her head and saw Kimo walking quickly toward them. She scrambled to her feet, wondering how he had found them.

"What are you doing here, Kimo?" she asked, her hands on her hips.

"It's Tutu."

"What's about her?"

"She needs you."

Lani dropped her hands. "Why?" she asked, concerned. "What's wrong with her?"

Kimo completely ignored Rhys. "I'll take you to her. She's in Queen's Hospital."

Torn between wanting to settle things between her and Rhys and wanting to rush to her grandmother, Lani looked at Rhys.

He held out his hand. "Give me your car keys. I'll follow you."

"There's no need for you to follow us," she said tightly, handing him the keys. "There isn't anything more we need to say to each other."

"The hell there isn't."

He started toward her, but Kimo stepped between them, his large body effectively blocking him.

Lani's voice was quiet but firm. "If you leave my car in the hotel parking lot, I'll have one of my cousins bring it back to me."

She turned abruptly and strode away, Kimo following her.

Seven

Instead of going to the emergency room when they reached the hospital, Kimo took Lani through the main lobby to the elevators. A few minutes later she glanced at her cousin as though he had lost his mind. He was taking her to the maternity ward.

Worried about her grandmother and still reeling from the conversation with Rhys on the beach, she wasn't in the mood for one of Kimo's practical jokes. "Did you take a wrong turn or something? What are we doing in the maternity ward? I thought you said Tutu was in the hospital."

"She is."

Holding her arm, he drew her into one of the rooms. The first bed was empty, but several people were sitting on it. One of them was Bianca. Quickly glancing around, Lani saw that all were members of her family. They greeted her and moved aside so she could approach the other bed. Bianca's sister was lying in it, and she gave Lani a pleased smile. In a chair at the foot of the bed was Emma Makena, looking fit and healthy.

Lani hugged Pami and asked all the appropriate questions about the baby, learning Pami now had a daughter named Emma.

As thrilled as Lani was about the baby, it was difficult for her to act normally in front of her family. She wanted to throttle Kimo for implying her grandmother was in the hospital because of an illness, not simply visiting a granddaugther.

After seeing the baby in the nursery along with everyone else, she was finally able to steer Kimo to one side of the hall away from the others.

"You have some explaining to do."

He held up his hand in a placating gesture. "I didn't lie to you. I said Tutu wanted to see you and that she was in the hospital."

"You made it sound urgent, and you did it on purpose. Why?"

He refused to meet Lani's angry eyes, his gaze flicking to a nurse walking by, then to a nurse's aid carrying flowers. "Tutu knew you would want to see Pami's baby."

"There was no rush. I didn't have to come to the hospital at that exact moment. I could see the baby and Pami tomorrow. Tell me why you really came after me."

Kimo still wouldn't look at her. He was a superb entertainer but not a very good liar. "Tutu asked me to find you, so I did."

"How did you know where I was?"

Now he looked at her, a slight smile curving his mouth. "You didn't fool Kome with the jaunt through the cane field. He phoned Tutu once he knew you were staying at Shark's Cove for a while."

"If Kome talked to Tutu, why didn't *he* come and tell me my grandmother wanted to see me? Why did you come instead? And please don't tell me you were in the neighborhood. I won't believe it because you never go near Shark's Cove."

Kimo sighed heavily. "Tutu wanted you away from the Englishman. It's that simple."

"You still haven't explained why you came for me and not Kome." A horrible suspicion began to grow. "Where is Kome?"

Kimo looked down at her, his expression one of apology. "Lani," he said hesitantly, "if you'd listened to Tutu in the beginning, none of this would have happened."

"None of what would have happened?" She clutched the front of his shirt. "What has Kome done with Rhys?"

Obviously angry at being put on the spot, Kimo spoke more roughly than usual. "He was warned off before, but it didn't do any good. Kome's going to put it a little stronger this time."

Lani felt sick. "Exactly what does that entail, Kimo? I swear if Kome hurts him, if there's a mark on him, I'll never forgive either one of you."

"Tutu asked us to only talk to him, convince him to move on to Australia or go back to England."

"And how is Kome going to do that? I remember how they persuaded that sailor to leave Laura alone. The man ended up in the hospital."

Kimo took her arm and started to lead her back toward Pami's room. "The best thing you can do is go home. Bianca will take you to your cottage. I have to get back to the club."

She pulled away from him. "I'm going to talk to Tutu. She can stop this."

Kimo grabbed her arm, his grip hard but not painful. "It won't do any good. You would only make matters worse. Tutu is trying to remove temptation from your path. She doesn't know how much you care for the Englishman yet. We haven't told her he has spent the night at your house. If you go running off to her, demanding he be left alone, she'll know."

Lani jerked her arm away again, but not so she could go speak to her grandmother. All she wanted to do was to get out of there and find Rhys. Because of her, he was being threatened, possibly physically. Kimo might sugarcoat it by saying Kome was only going to talk to Rhys, but Bianca's brother was not known for his even temper. If Rhys didn't take him seriously and said the wrong thing, he could be hurt.

"Just go home, Maia," Kimo said quietly.

Will Rhys be there?"

"No."

Sounding calmer than she felt, she asked, "Will he be in his hotel room?"

Kimo looked away. "I don't know. That's the truth, Maia. All I know is Kome phoned me at the club and said Tutu wanted me to go to Shark's Cove to take you to the hospital. He had to get the Englishman alone in order to talk to him, to persuade him to leave the island."

"And if he isn't successful?"

Kimo didn't answer her question. Instead, he put his hands on her shoulders to hold her directly in front of him. "Kome doesn't know the Englishman has spent the night at your cottage. All I've told him is the Englishman is still seeing you."

Lani knew she should be relieved for that small blessing, but she was still concerned about Rhys.

Bianca left the nursery window and approached them. "Are you about ready to go, Lani? We're all leaving so Pami can get some rest."

"I'm ready."

Kimo put his hand on her arm as she started to turn away. "I'm sorry, Maia."

She nodded. "It's not your fault."

As they rode down in the elevator Bianca asked, "What isn't Kimo's fault?"

"Your brother is having a heart-to-heart talk with Rhys, hopefully not a fist-to-fist chat. If he had just waited, he would have seen that none of this was necessary. I won't be seeing Rhys again."

Bianca looked at her with concern in her eyes, but didn't comment or ask any questions. Lani knew why. Her cousin probably knew more about the situation than she did.

Lani was quiet during the ride to her cottage. She didn't press Bianca for information concerning Rhys's whereabouts. It was doubtful Bianca would know that.

When they arrived at her cottage, her car was in the driveway. There were no lights on inside. Bianca asked if Lani wanted her to come in, but Lani shook her head.

"No." Opening the door, she added, "Thanks for the ride."

Before Lani shut the door, Bianca called out, "Lani, are you going to be all right?"

Lani's mouth twisted into a poor imitation of a smile. "I'll let you know."

After Bianca backed out of her driveway, Lani checked her car and wasn't surprised to find the keys in the ignition. The picnic hamper was sitting on the backseat, its lid closed. At least Kome had been tidy. When she entered her cottage, she wasn't surprised to find it empty. She hadn't expected Rhys to be there, but she couldn't help being disappointed anyway.

In her bedroom she glanced at the bed, then quickly away. Opening her closet, she took out a pair of jeans and a long-sleeved shirt. They were going to be too hot, but it was either swelter or be cut by the foliage she was going to be walking through.

If she had any sense, she would wait until morning to look for Rhys. But why should tonight be any different? she asked herself. Her track record for the past week wouldn't warrant a passing grade on any intelligence test.

After changing her clothes, she hunted around in the kitchen for a flashlight, finally finding one in the last drawer she opened. There were several places she thought Kome might have taken Rhys, and none of them was on a well-lighted street.

He could have taken Rhys directly to the airport, but Lani didn't think so. There were his clothes, his passport, and his airline ticket still in his hotel room in Waikiki. She couldn't imagine Rhys calmly letting Kome escort him to his room to pack his clothes so that Kome could then drive him to the airport. Kome would take Rhys somewhere private to have his little chat.

Lani had a few ideas where to look. As children, she and her cousins had gone to a number of places on the island where only the locals went. Those were the areas where she would start.

A little after midnight she was about to give up. Even though she hadn't seen Kome's Jeep anywhere near each area, she had tramped through thick undergrowth of ferns, vines, and flowering shrubs to waterfalls, shacks, and old camping sites. Without any success. She was running out of places to go.

There was one more stop she could make. It was a long shot but the last place she could think of Kome going. Sea Life Park at Makapuu Point was a popular tourist attraction, where tourists could see an ocean science theater, performing dolphins, and an assortment of reef fish and other sea life. The evening show was over at ten o'clock, so the park would be closed. Since Kome worked at the park, he might choose it as a place to take Rhys.

She strained her eyes to examine each car that passed her as on she drove to the park, hoping to see Kome's Jeep. Several miles after passing Haunauma Bay and the Blow Hole, she saw a man walking alongside the road. He was dressed in tan slacks and a white shirt and had sandy-colored hair. Relieved, she slammed on her brakes and pulled off the pavement. Rhys stopped walking when he spotted the car. He raised his hand to shield his eyes from the glare of her headlights, his stance stiff and guarded.

Lani opened her door and got out. "Rhys! It's me, Lani."

Lowering his hand, he walked toward her. As he got closer she could see he looked as he did earlier on the beach. There were no signs of any violence on his clothing or his face. The wind, rather than his having been manhandled by her cousins, could be responsible for his hair being mussed. At least, she hoped it was the wind.

"Are you all right?" she asked.

"Oh, I'm just fine," he said tightly, stopping a foot away from her. "There's nothing I like better than an evening stroll when I have no notion where I'm going."

She heard the anger in his voice and really couldn't blame him. She could apologize. She could give him excuses for her family's behavior. But no explanation would change the last several hours, so she offered none.

"Get in," she said. "I'll drive you back to your hotel."

He shook his head. "You get in. I'll drive. I've gone for one ride tonight with someone else driving, and I wasn't wild about where I ended up."

She walked around the front of the car and opened the passenger door. He got in the driver's side and waited until she had fastened her seat belt before pulling back onto the road.

His hands were tight on the steering wheel, and he wondered if he should be driving. With each step he had taken along that road, his anger had grown into blinding fury. He hadn't liked the threats of broken bones, nor the helpless feeling of being dumped on the side of the road.

"You'll have to tell me where to go," he said, forcing his tense shoulders to relax. "Your charming cousin blindfolded me, so I haven't the faintest idea where I am."

"There's a place up ahead where you can turn around."

As they passed Diamond Head before reaching Waikiki Lani said quietly, "If it's any consolation, I was taken for a ride tonight, too. In more ways than one. When we reached the hospital, Kimo took me to the maternity ward to see my cousin who just had a baby. Tutu was there, but she was fine."

"Your family has a peculiar sense of humor."

"You're not laughing."

He slanted a glance at her, then returned his attention to the road. His temper had cooled somewhat, although anger still shimmered within him. "I didn't think it was very funny."

"What happened after I left?"

"A large man who I assume is one of your cousins stopped me as I was getting into your car. Straight out of a rather bad movie, he said we were going for a little ride. Since there was two other men with him, I didn't have much choice but to do as he said. He blindfolded me, although I was spared having my wrists shackled. If you've never ridden in a Jeep with your eyes covered, you haven't lived. The man's driving ability is on par with his charm. Neither is very comfortable."

"I don't need to ask what he wanted. He told you to stay away from me, didn't he?"

"Basically. He made a few threats, not at all subtle, and told me to get on the next flight off the island. There were several words I didn't understand, and there was one he kept repeating. It sounded like pow, as in the affair between you and me was pow."

"Pau," she murmured, spelling it for him. "It means finished, ended. He's right. It is."

Rhys's head jerked around, his jaw clenching. "The hell it is. If you believe that, you're as crazy as the rest of your family."

When they reached Waikiki, he turned into the entrance to the Outrigger Hotel. After parking the car, he got out and came around to open her door. Taking it for granted she would be going home, she held out her hand. Instead of giving her the keys, he clasped her hand and began walking away from the car, drawing her along with him.

She had to walk quickly in order to keep up with him as he crossed Kalakaua Avenue and entered the International Place. This time she didn't have to ask where they were going.

Keeping her hand firmly in his, Rhys entered Trader Vic's. The floor show was over, and they found Kimo in the bar having a drink. Rhys released her hand, and slipped his arm around her waist, holding her clamped to his side as he stopped directly in front of Kimo.

Under other circumstances, Lani would have found Kimo's expression funny. He couldn't have looked more stunned if a coconut had fallen on his head. He looked from Rhys to her, then to the possessive arm around her waist.

Rhys's voice was casual. The expression in his eyes was not. "If my little jaunt this evening was your idea, you should know it didn't work. I'm going to continue seeing Lani whether you, your grandmother, and half of the island like it or not. You'd better get more men and they'd better be bigger. I'll be ready for them next time."

Without giving Kimo a chance to say anything, Rhys turned and left, taking Lani with him. He didn't speak again until he had unlocked the door to his hotel room. Inside the room, he leaned against the closed door and looked at her.

"No matter what I say, it's not going to make any difference with your family, is it?"

"I did try to warn you, Rhys."

"Several times." He walked past her and stood in front of the window. "It was becoming boring."

She looked at his profile, silhouetted against the darkness outside the window. His hands were stuffed into his pockets, his back stiff. He was still furious. She couldn't blame him if he wanted to vent some of his rage on her. After all, it was because of her he had been left to find his way back to his hotel on foot.

Walking slowly toward him, she asked, "What are you going to do?"

He continued to stare out the window. "If you had asked that after your cousins had left me beside the road, I would have said I wanted revenge."

"And now?"

He turned. "What I want hasn't changed. I want you."

"Rhys," she said wearily, "we've been through all this. I thought you understood. It's not going to work out between us."

"I've heard all your reasons. Some made sense

and some are pure rubbish." Leaving the window, Rhys walked across the room to her. He kept his hands in his pockets to keep from reaching for her and shaking her. She kept putting up roadblocks instead of trying to clear a path.

He stopped in front of her. "You've told me why it wouldn't work between us, why your family wants to get rid of me, and a lot of other hogwash." He leaned forward until his nose was almost touching hers. "The one thing you haven't told me is why you've slept with me."

She backed away quickly. Panic welled up inside her, making it difficult to breathe. "What difference does that make? We still have the same problems we had earlier. I live here. You live in England. That's great if we want to be pen pals. Under the circumstances, there's no way we could be anything else."

He came after her, as relentless in his pursuit as he was in his questions. "You've slept with me. Why?"

She took another step away. Turning his question back on him, she countered, "Why did you sleep with me?"

He straightened, still holding her gaze with his own. "Because I'm in love with you."

She stared at him, too astonished to speak or even think.

A corner of his mouth curved upward. He lifted her chin with one finger to close her parted lips. "Does the fact that I love you really come as all that much of a shock, Lani?"

"It's the last thing I thought you would say."

His thumb stroked her bottom lip. "And you aren't sure you want to hear it."

She couldn't think when he was touching her. Moving away from him, she wrapped her arms around her waist. "It would have been better if you hadn't told me."

This time he didn't come after her. "Denying feelings doesn't change them. You have a right to know." He paused, then added, "Just as I have a right to know how you feel."

She drew a deep steadying breath into her tortured lungs. It didn't help. "You don't play fair," she murmured.

Anger flickered in his eyes. "Let's not get into a discussion of fairness, Lani. The last couple of hours haven't been fair. The way your family considers me a threat isn't fair." His hands closed over her shoulders. "It isn't fair for you to tell me to get the hell out of your life when you love me."

She flinched as though he had struck her. "How do you—I never said—"

His fingers loosened their hold. He slid his hands down her arms, surprised to find her own hands were cold. "There's a difference between having sex and making love. I never knew there was until we went to bed together. I don't believe you could respond to me as you do if you didn't care for me." He brought her hands up to his chest, his eyes holding hers. "I don't believe you would have gone to bed with me unless you care for me."

She could admit her feelings to herself but not to him. Once she said the words aloud, once he heard them, there would be no going back. Her arguments would be worthless.

She freed herself and walked stiffly to the couch, sinking heavily onto the cushions. "I don't know what happens now."

Rhys was disappointed but didn't push. He crossed the room and sat down beside her. "Your cousin's actions tonight have forced things to move faster than they might have otherwise. We're going to have to make some decisions."

"Like what?"

"Whether to have your grandmother over for dinner on Friday night or Saturday night."

She whirled around to face him. "Are you crazy? Why would we invite my grandmother to dinner?"

He kicked off his shoes, then placed his feet on the coffee table and rested his head on the back of the couch. "She's prejudiced against me, and she doesn't even know me. We're going to correct that. I'm British, the same as your father, but that's the only thing we have in common. I won't be painted with the same brush by your grandmother just because I coincidentally come from the same country as the man who abandoned her daughter."

Lani slumped back against the couch. It had been a long strange day, and it wasn't over. "I don't understand why you're doing all this. Confronting Kimo at Trader Vic's? Having my grandmother over for dinner? You're going to stir a hornet's nest into a frenzy, then hop on a plane, leaving me to fight off the stings."

Moving swiftly, he reached for her and lifted her onto his lap. "It's amazing how an intelligent woman can be so dense."

Holding her pressed against his chest, he stretched his other arm across her thighs. The feel of her firm breasts almost made him forget everything except how good it was to have her in his arms.

Lani wished she could just lose herself in the sensuality Rhys wove around her. But she couldn't. That was what she had done too many times before when they should have been talking.

"I must be incredibly stupid," she said, "because I don't know the answers to the questions I just asked you."

His hand began to stroke her thigh. "You're very innocent." A corner of his mouth twitched when he saw her raise a brow. "Well, maybe not technically. You've been around men all your life, but you don't really know much about how they think or why they do certain things a certain way."

She moved her hips slightly, stroking the hard bulge pressed against her. "Tell me what men think and why they do certain things a certain way."

He closed his eyes as a shaft of desire stabbed through him. It hadn't been such a good idea to pull her onto his lap after all. She needed explanations, not him crawling all over her.

Opening his eyes, he looked into hers. Shining green eyes a man could drown in. "You're making it very hard for me to concentrate on this conversation."

She smiled provocatively at his choice of words, and coiled her arms tighter around his neck. Because of him, she had discovered a sensuality within herself she hadn't known existed. It was one of the gifts he had unknowingly given her. Before she had known him, she had been like a budding flower, unaware of her own potential until he had made her burst into full bloom as a mature, complete woman.

"No other woman has made me feel like you do," he said, his voice low and husky. "All I have to do is touch you and my body goes up in flames. I never missed feeling this way before because I never knew anything this magical, this powerful. Now I know what it's like and I don't want to lose it or you. I want us to be together, Lani. Whether it's in Australia or England or Timbuktu. The place isn't important. What we have is. I need to know if it's what you want."

She stared at him, unsure what to say, when there was a loud persistent knock on the door.

Rhys's first impulse was to ignore it. He hadn't ordered anything from room service, and he certainly wasn't expecting any company. It was probably someone who had the wrong room. But whoever it was wasn't giving up and was becoming impatient.

A muffled male voice came through the door. "Jones, open this door. I need to talk to Lani."

Lani recognized the voice before Rhys did. "It's Kimo."

Eight

She was abruptly set aside as Rhys sprang to his feet. "He'd better have a damn good reason for this."

In a few strides he was at the door. He flicked off the locks and yanked it open. Kimo took one step back instinctively, holding up his hands when he saw Rhys's less than hospitable expression.

"It isn't what you think. I'm not here to harass you. I need to speak to Lani. Her grandmother has had an accident."

"You've already used that one, Kimo," Lani said, coming up behind Rhys. "Can't you be more original?"

"This time I'm telling the truth. Auntie Mei was driving her home from the hospital, and they were hit by a drunk driver. Both of them were injured." He looked from Lani to Rhys. "I'm telling the truth. I just got a phone call at the club from Loke." For Rhys's benefit, he explained, "Loke is a policeman who heard the call at the station. He doesn't know how serious the injuries are. All he could tell me was there had been a car accident, and Tutu and

Auntie Mei were being taken by ambulance to Queen's Hospital."

Lani believed him. "All right. I'll come with you."

As she passed Rhys he took her arm. "I'm coming, too."

"We could be there all night," she said, adding ruefully, "What's left of the night."

"I'm coming," he repeated. "The last time you took off with him, I ended up stranded halfway around the island. Besides, your family might as well get used to seeing me with you."

Kimo's dark eyes widened at Rhys's last remark, but apparently he decided this wasn't the time to ask the Englishman what he meant.

When they arrived at the hospital, they joined several other members of the family in the waiting room. Emma and Auntie Mei were being treated in the emergency room, and there was still no word on how serious the injuries were. Other people trickled into the waiting room as the news spread through the Makena clan. Those with younger children had remained at home, but there were still enough people to fill the room.

When Rhys sat down beside Lani, he was aware of the curious stares from some of her relatives. No one, though, expressed surprise or hostility at his presence. Except Kome when he arrived. As he entered the waiting room he stopped abruptly the moment he saw the man he thought he had scared away from Lani. He blinked several times as though he couldn't quite believe what he was seeing.

The dumbfounded expression on the other man's face gave Rhys a small amount of satisfaction. He would have enjoyed Kome's consternation more if he weren't feeling the onset of a migraine. The strain of the long, unusual day was catching up with him.

Part of the tension he was feeling was due to what he needed to ask of Lani. He knew she cared deeply for her family, but it hadn't occurred to him until now just how difficult it would be for her to leave them. *If* she agreed to leave them.

Ever since they had arrived at the hospital, she had gone from relative to relative, giving what comfort she could. It pleased him that she always returned to sit beside him, never forgetting he was there. Her family was important to her, but she made it clear he was, too. She was going to have to make a choice between them, and soon. It remained to be seen which she would choose.

Lani was turning away from consoling an aunt and saw Rhys lean his head against the wall behind his chair. His eyes were closed, but she could see the tension in his jaw and across his forehead.

She laid her hand on his arm. "Rhys?"

He didn't open his eyes. "Hmmm?"

"Why don't you go back to your hotel? This could take all night."

"Are you staying?"

"Yes. I have to. She's my grandmother."

He reached up, unerringly finding her hand without opening his eyes, then brought their clasped hands to his thigh. "If you're staying, so am I."

Her fingers tightened around his. "Rhys, if you're starting to get one of your headaches, you should rest before it gets worse."

He opened his eyes, seeing the concern on her face. A corner of his mouth lifted slowly. "I'm all right. You're losing as much sleep as I am."

She knew Rhys wouldn't want her to fuss over him. She could suggest he take his medication, except the last time she'd seen the bottle, it was on the windowsill in her kitchen. There wasn't anything else she could do but wait for the news about her grandmother.

It wasn't any easier for anyone else to wait. Each minute ticked slowly past on the large clock on the wall until at 3:00 A.M., Kimo's patience ran out. He went looking for answers and, within fifteen minutes, came back with them.

Addressing the room at large, he announced, "Tutu and Auntie Mei have been taken to their rooms and won't be allowed visitors until later this morning."

He had to hold up his hand to still the many questions fired at him from all directions. "Let me finish. Tutu has a broken ankle and a sprained wrist. Auntie Mei has a broken hip and a broken arm. Both have bruises, but the doctors have assured me they will recover quickly. They are going to have to stay in the hospital for a few days." Glancing up at the clock, he added, "I suggest we all go home and get some rest."

Lani tugged at Rhys's hand. "We can leave now. There's nothing more we can do here."

He pushed himself out of the chair and stayed beside her as she said good-bye to her relatives. He was surprised when he was included in the farewells. Several of Lani's uncles and cousins shook his hand, and one of her aunts wrapped her plump arms around him in an enthusiastic embrace. The fact that he had remained with Lani throughout the long wait at that hour of the night had changed a few opinions in his favor.

As they left the hospital his arm automatically encircled her waist, his gesture possessive and natural. "I know you have to go to work later this morning, but I'd like for you to stay at the hotel rather than drive home. I don't feel like driving all the way back to your cottage at this hour."

She could have argued that she could drive herself, but exhaustion had caught up with her, too.

She smiled at him. "I don't have a nightgown."

He returned the provocative smile. "You won't need one."

Rhys was still sleeping when Lani dragged the sheet away and slipped her legs over the side of the bed. Her brain felt as though it was wrapped in cotton batting. Two hours of sleep hadn't been nearly enough.

As soon as they had returned to his room, they'd barely had the energy to remove their clothing before falling into bed. Rhys had drawn her against him and fallen quickly into a deep sleep. Lani had meant to ask him if there was anything she could do for his headache, but as soon as she felt his solid warmth along her slender body, her eyes had closed.

The sun was just beginning to throw light around the edges of the drapes drawn over the windows. She didn't need to turn on one of the lamps on either side of the bed in order to see where she was going. The thick carpet muffled her footsteps as she walked over to his closet to take one of his shirts off a hanger. Slipping it on, she turned toward the bathroom but was stopped by the sound of a husky, sleepy voice.

"Come back to bed. It's the middle of the night."

She glanced over at the bed and saw Rhys leaning on an elbow, the sheet bunched at his waist.

"It's a little after six," she said.

"That's the middle of the night."

"I need to go back to the cottage." She glanced down at the shirt she was holding closed in front. "I can't very well wear this to work."

His gaze lowered to the shirt she was wearing, recognizing it. "I've worn that shirt to work and no one complained."

She smiled. "I think my bank manager would," she said as she started toward the bathroom.

As she passed him he swiftly reached for her arm. In one smooth motion she was tumbled onto the bed.

"I think I will complain about the shirt after all. It covers you too well."

He kissed her lazily, enjoying the feel of her under him. He was becoming addicted to waking up with her, to feeling her pliant body against his. He skimmed away his shirt, needing to caress her silky skin.

Lani didn't even try to resist the magic he conjured up with each kiss, each stroke of his hands. She clutched his shoulders as she fell into the whirlpool of passion that was both new and familiar. She was helpless against the demands he made on her body, yet had never felt stronger as a woman.

Lani didn't wake Rhys before she left the room. She drove to her cottage, quickly showered and changed, then got back into her car to make the return trip. By the time she sat down at her desk, she felt as though she had put in a full day, and it was only nine o'clock.

She went to the hospital during her lunch hour to visit her grandmother and her aunt. Two cups of coffee, which she wasn't used to drinking, had left her nerves a bit jangly. They weren't calmed a bit by the barrage of questions fired by her grandmother almost as soon as she entered the hospital room.

"Is it true, Lani? Are you still seeing the *haole* from England?"

Lani leaned down to kiss her grandmother's cheek. "Hello, Tutu. I guess I don't need to ask how you are feeling."

"You haven't answered my question."

She pulled up a chair, marveling at her grandmother's recuperative powers. Even a foot in a cast and her wrist wrapped heavily in an elastic bandage didn't diminish any of the older woman's spirit.

"His name is Rhys Jones, Tutu. Yes, I'm still seeing him. Could we talk about something else? How are you feeling?"

Emma didn't want to talk about the accident or her injuries. "This is not good, child. This will only bring pain."

"Tutu, I'm not a child. I'm old enough to make my own decisions about who I see. If my choices bring me pain, then I have only myself to blame. If you do anything to take my right to choose away from me, the blame will be yours, not mine."

"The pain can be avoided if you stay away from that man. I've tried to protect you, but you won't listen. What I've done is for your own good."

"I know you believe that. I suppose after what happened to my mother, I can understand why you feel so strongly about my seeing Rhys." She saw her grandmother's eyes darken with pain that was as fresh as it had been twenty-four years ago. "I'm sorry, Tutu. I know you don't like to talk about my mother and what happened to her."

The older woman frowned. "No, I don't like to think about it. Your mother was abandoned by that man and died of a broken heart. It would kill me if the same happened to you."

Lani got out of her chair and leaned over the

bed. Placing her hand on her grandmother's arm, she said, "I'm not my mother, Tutu. You have to trust me to do what I think is best for me."

"And this man is what's best for you?"

Lani didn't know how to answer that. Her relationship with Rhys was a variety of things, but *best* wasn't one of the words she would use to describe it.

Emma waited for an answer. When none came, she asked, "Exactly what is going on between you? Is it serious?"

The questions weren't getting any easier, Lani thought ruefully. She left the side of the bed and walked over to the window. "He's very important to me, Tutu." She gave her grandmother a wry smile over her shoulder. "He's also temporary. He'll be leaving any day now."

"I do not want him to take you with him. He could promise to let you come back for a visit but he would be lying."

Something in her grandmother's voice had Lani turning to face her. "You don't even know him. Why do you think he would be lying?"

Emma lifted her chin defiantly. "He is the same type of man as your father. Richard McGregor lied. He said he would be back for Lahela, but he never came. When she wrote to tell him about you, his mother sent a check." She made a rude sound. "I sent it back."

Lani returned to the bed. "Why didn't my mother go to England with Richard McGregor? I've always wondered. Her place should have been with her husband."

"No!" Emma snapped, her eyes flashing with anger as she sat upright. "Her place was here on this island." Leaning back, she said in a calmer voice, "Lahela was a child of the sun. She wouldn't have been happy in that cold foreign country, away from everyone who loved her. She belonged here. I told him that. He agreed with me."

Lani didn't debate the issue any further. Her suspicions had been verified. Her grandmother had been responsible for keeping her mother on the island, refusing to let her go, perhaps forever, to another land away from her family. She could understand why Emma had done it. Emma's family was her whole life. To lose a child was to lose a piece of herself, so she had held on tightly to her daughter—as she was attempting to hold on to her.

Lani bent over to kiss her grandmother's cheek. "I have to get back to work." Raising her head, she saw the concern still in the older woman's eyes. "I'm not going anywhere, Tutu." Mainly because she hadn't been asked, she thought with regret. "You concentrate on getting well and try to stop worrying about me."

After a short visit to her aunt's room, Lani left the hospital and returned to the bank. Throughout the afternoon she found herself thinking about the conversation with her grandmother. And about Rhys. She had reassured her grandmother that she wouldn't be leaving the island with Rhys, but she hadn't told her why.

Lani felt as though she were sitting on a fence, and it wasn't a comfortable position. She wasn't sure which side she was going to end up on. She had talked to her grandmother about choices, but whether she had a future with Rhys wasn't a decision that was only hers to make. He seemed to enjoy being with her. His desire for her hadn't waned. If anything, he appeared to want her more than he had at the beginning. Their physical relationship wasn't the problem.

His imminent departure was. At least, it was for her.

She could tell herself a hundred times that there was no future with Rhys, that she should cherish the time she had with him now because that was all there was going to be. It didn't stop her from wanting more.

Before leaving the bank for the day, she phoned Rhys's hotel room. On the second ring a man answered, but it wasn't Rhys.

"Excuse me, I must have misdialed." She gave the number of Rhys's room and was told that she'd called the correct room. The man and his wife had just checked into the hotel and had been given that room. Lani disconnected the call and redialed the hotel. The hotel clerk was helpful, telling her that Mr. Jones had checked out of his room around two o'clock.

The drive to her cottage seemed to take forever. She discovered that the theory about caffeine alleviating the need for sleep was highly overrated. All the coffee had done was set her nerves on edge, jangling them like cheap tin bells. Her eyes felt as though her lids were coated with sand, and her brain was chugging along in low gear.

Which was probably why she didn't notice that putting her key in her front door hadn't been necessary. Or it could have been because of the overwhelming disappointment she felt when Rhys wasn't waiting on her doorstep.

Hearing that he had checked out of his hotel had numbed her already exhausted mind. No matter how many times she had told herself he would be leaving, now that it had actually happened, she couldn't deal with it. At least not yet. Not when she was so tired. All she wanted to do was close her eyes and reach for the blessed oblivion of sleep.

She closed the door and leaned wearily against it, then willed her leaden feet to move in the direction of her bedroom. She never made it. The couch was much closer. She yawned as she kicked off her shoes, then removed her suit jacket. The plump cushions of the couch accepted her weight, and she groaned softly. Two seconds after her head hit the decorative pillow, she was asleep.

She wasn't sure what woke her. She couldn't recall hearing a sound, although that didn't mean there hadn't been one. Maybe it was the ceiling fan overhead, slowly stirring the air. She didn't remember turning it on.

Frowning, she slid her legs over the side of the couch and stood up. A quick glance around the room showed her everything was as it always had been. As groggy as she had been when she arrived home, she might have turned the fan on herself and just didn't remember doing it.

After she took a shower and changed into a white bikini, she wrapped a length of material around her hips, knotting it on one side. She walked into the kitchen to get Tommy so she could take him down to the beach.

His aquarium was empty.

There was no way he could have gotten out by himself, but she looked around the table and on the floor anyway just in case. He wasn't anywhere to be seen. Then she noticed the inner back door was open. Bianca and Kimo each had a key to her cottage, but they had never used them. Neither one had ever entered her house when she wasn't home, or taken her turtle. Still, there was a first time for everything.

Figuring the beach was the likeliest place to find her unknown guest and Tommy, she opened the screen door and stepped out onto the back porch. She stopped abruptly when she saw the figure of a man down by the water.

Dressed in his cutoff jeans and an aloha shirt open down the front, Rhys was looking down at the sand. She blinked, wondering if he was a mirage, but he was still there when she opened her eyes. As she walked slowly toward him she could see a dark object on the sand. Shaking her head in bemusement, she realized Rhys was taking Tommy for his evening stroll.

Rhys looked up and saw her when she was about ten feet away. Her hair blew gently around her face, and the graceful swing of her hips was accentuated by the lavalava draped below her waist. She was like an exotic blossom thriving in the sultry tropical air, infinitely touchable and dramatically beautiful. He could only hope she would accept moving away from Hawaii . . . with him.

He waited for her to come to him. When she stopped a foot away, he reached out to cup the back of her neck and bring her closer. Lowering his head, he gave her an intimate kiss of welcome and promise.

When she didn't respond, he eased back from her. His gaze roamed over her face, seeing the strain around her eyes. "Did you have a rough day?"

She took a step back, needing the distance, however slight, between them. "I called your hotel. They said you had checked out."

He heard the hurt in her voice, saw it reflected in her eyes. He could only imagine what she had thought. "I did."

She opened her mouth but couldn't decide which question to ask first. There were so many. Shaking her head in bewilderment, she sat down on the sand, near Tommy. She wrapped her arms tightly around her knees and kept her gaze on the turtle as he slowly plodded along the beach.

Rhys's arm brushed her thigh as he sat down beside her. "Kimo drove me here and let me in with his key."

Her eyes were wide, and she was more confused than ever as she turned to stare at him. "Kimo? Why did you ask Kimo? I would have given you my key if you'd asked for it."

"There wasn't time. I didn't decide to check out until this afternoon. Besides, I needed to talk to your cousin."

She sprang to her knees and knelt in front of him. "Why? Did Kome bother you again?"

The material wrapped around her hips had parted, exposing her supple thigh. Forcing his attention away from that expanse of tanned skin, he said, "No one has been bothering me. There were a few things I needed to get settled with Kimo, so I called Trader Vic's. Luckily he was there and could get away when I told him what I wanted to talk to him about."

"I don't understand why you checked out of the hotel. Have you come to say good-bye? You checked out because you're leaving?"

"I'm not here to say good-bye. I'm going to be staying with Kimo. We agreed it was the right thing to do under the circumstances." He saw her frown in bewilderment and explained further, "Kimo and I have come to an understanding."

That was more than she had, she mused. Anger filtered through the jumble of emotions within her and rose to the top. "Do you have any idea of what you just put me through? I thought you'd left. Without even saying good-bye. The hotel clerk had more consideration for me than you did!"

"Lani, you should know me well enough by now

to realize I wouldn't have left the island without you."

"I didn't think you would leave yet, which is why I was so shocked when I heard you had checked out."

His own anger flared at her use of the word *yet*. She still expected him to leave her eventually. He held her by the shoulders, forcing her to look at him. "Lani, I'm going to say this very slowly and very clearly. If you need it in writing, I'll write it down. If you want it etched in stone, I'll even do that. I love you. I'm not leaving here without you. I've been on the telephone most of the day making arrangements so we can be together. That's one of the reasons I wanted to talk to Kimo."

She stared at him. "Maybe it's your accent that makes it hard for me to understand what you're talking about."

His grip tightened, his fingers digging into her warm flesh enough to hold her, but not hard enough to hurt her.

"Lani, do you want us to be together?"

She didn't hesitate. "Yes. But—"

"Do you love me?"

Her answer came out as soft as a sigh. "Yes."

"Say it."

Her eyes flashed with temper. "I love you, but—"

He had heard all he needed to hear. Drawing her to him, he kissed her tenderly. His instincts had told him she loved him, but it was wonderful to hear her say the words aloud. It was necessary. For both of them.

Releasing her abruptly, he scooped up the turtle before getting to his feet. Extending his hand down to her, he said, "Let's put Tommy back in his basin. Then I'll tell you some of the plans I've made."

Taking his hand, she let him pull her up. "If

you've already made the plans, what's there to discuss?"

He tightened his grip on her fingers in case she tried to pull away. "I thought you might like a little input in planning your own wedding."

Nine

Lani's breath stopped. Finally managing to draw air into her lungs, she asked, "My what?"

"Your wedding. Our wedding."

His words tumbled over and over in her mind, but for the life of her she couldn't sort them out enough for them to make any sense.

Rhys went on when she didn't say anything. "I've discussed it with Kimo, and he said you would want the ceremony here. My mother and sister are flying in from Australia. My partners will be arriving at the end of the week. Aku will get the pig and gather a crew together to dig something he called an *imu* to roast the pig in. Kimo is contacting a couple of your aunts who will organize the luau for after the ceremony."

"Wait a minute!" she said desperately. "You're going too fast."

Suddenly serious, he brought his hands up to frame her face. "If anything, I'm not going fast enough. We're running out of time, darling. I can't stay here much longer. You'll just have to keep up the best you can."

She sighed. "You're going to have to spare a few minutes while I try to sort out everything. A short time ago I thought you had already left. Now you say the word *wedding* as though I know what you're talking about. It sounds as if you've discussed this with everyone on the island but me." Her voice rose. "We've never discussed getting married. We've never said anything about the future."

"That doesn't mean I haven't been thinking about it. When a man and a woman love each other, they find a way to be together. It's not unheard of for two people to get married under those circumstances." His mouth curved in a wry smile. "Especially when there are a number of large cousins in the background who would take exception to the couple living together."

She was actually beginning to believe him. "Could you slow down enough to go through the motions of actually asking me to marry you? I've heard that's how it's usually done."

Her spirited request amused him, but he sobered as he said, "You need to know that if you agree to marry me, it will mean leaving your home, your family, and your friends. That might not be fair, but it's the way it has to be. I don't think you would be happy in London, so I've made other plans. You're a woman of warmth and sunshine, not cold and fog. My partners in London have agreed to my suggestion to open a law office in Melbourne."

Lani thought of how her grandmother had described her mother. Tutu had said she was a child of the sun. Now Rhys was saying basically the same thing about her.

Anxiety and impatience were overflowing in Rhys. So far he had been doing all the talking, and Lani continued to stare at him as though he were speaking some foreign language.

"Lani, talk to me. Am I asking too much?"

"You haven't asked me anything yet."

Being unsure of her answer made the question the hardest he'd ever had to ask. "Anne Kapiolani Makena McGregor, will you marry me?"

He barely had time to brace himself before she flung herself at him, her arms going around his neck. "Yes," she breathed. Practically shouting, she said again, "Yes!"

Holding her tightly, he whirled her around several times. The relief was overpowering. When he lowered her bare feet to the sand, he looked down at her. "Are you sure, Lani? I know I'm asking you to make all the sacrifices, but I promise we will come back to Hawaii as often as possible."

"I would rather be with you in Australia, England, or Timbuktu, than by myself in Hawaii. It's true I've never lived anywhere else, but that doesn't mean I can't be happy away from here. Home will be wherever you are."

Her words electrified him, sending a current of joy through him. As much as he wanted to revel in the knowledge that she would be his forever, he had to bring them both down to earth. There were still a few problems in their way.

"Your grandmother isn't going to agree with that."

Lani felt as though she had been offered a gift, only to have it yanked away. She dropped her arms and walked over to pick up the turtle who had wandered too close to the water. Carrying him, she returned to Rhys.

"We'd better go over those plans you've made."

Rhys lifted her chin. "We'll work everything out, Lani."

She wrapped her fingers around his wrist. "I know." She smiled faintly. "I just realized how complicated it was going to be."

"The wedding or the marriage?" he asked quietly.

She refused to conjure up demons that could ruin the day she had been given her greatest chance at happiness. She didn't want to think about her grandmother's reaction, nor all the other problems ahead of them. For now, she wanted to rejoice in the knowledge that she would be spending the rest of her life with the man she loved.

They would have to face the problems soon enough.

Smiling up at him, she said lightly, "I was just wondering what we're going to do about Tommy."

He took the turtle from her. "That's not a problem. I'll adopt him."

Laughing, Lani walked beside him back to the cottage. If only all their problems could be solved as easily as that.

After Tommy had been returned to his aquarium, Lani sat down and watched the turtle munch on the food she had left for him that morning. She felt dazed and needed a few minutes to gather her wits about her. It was as though she had been on an emotional roller coaster and it was time to get off and find solid ground.

Rhys pulled out the chair opposite her. "You have one week."

"For what?"

"Before we leave the island."

He expected her to protest, but not to lower her head on top of her folded arms on the table. He started to ask her what was wrong, then stopped when he saw her shoulders shaking. His chair scraped against the floor as he shoved it back.

Hunkering down beside her, he touched her arm. "Lani? Darling, don't cry. We'll work it out. Whatever it is, we'll work it out."

When she raised her head, he was in for another shock. She was laughing. Silently, but definitely laughing. The moment she saw his face, she didn't bother to hide her amusement any longer. Rhys sat back on his heels, a frown creasing his brow.

"What in bloody hell is wrong with you? What's so damn funny?" he asked crossly.

"You are."

He stood up and set his hands on his hips. "Thank you very much," he said huffily.

Lani managed to control herself. "It's going to take a little getting used to."

"What is?"

"Living with a tsunami."

He blinked. "I've been called a lot of things since I arrived on Oahu. I don't recall that one."

"It's a large tidal wave." She rose from her chair and placed her hands on his chest. "You swept into my life, wiping everything out of your path. If there's an obstacle in your way, you knock it down or go over it."

He gripped her waist. "Lani, I can't tell if you're complaining or pleased. Dammit, talk to me. Tell me what's going on in that head of yours."

"Why? You haven't been interested before."

"Ah, I see. Are we about to have a discussion on equality?"

"It's as a good a time as any. I might have given the impression I take life as it comes. To a large extent, I guess I do. Loving you has made some major changes in my life, and there are going to be many more. I would like to be a part of the decisions concerning those changes."

"I'm sorry. My only excuse is I've wanted you so desperately, and the clock was ticking by so rapidly, I just charged ahead on my own."

Taking her hand, he drew her into the living room. He gestured for her to sit, joining her as soon as she was settled on the couch. "I'll tell you what I've arranged so far. Jump in when you hear something you don't like."

Lani had few complaints once she had heard the plans Rhys had made. He had taken care of everything except giving notice at her bank. That she would do on Monday. She would have liked to have given more than a week's notice, but that was all the time she had. The wedding was scheduled for the following Saturday, with their departure from the island set for Monday.

There was little time for her to dwell on leaving her home and her family. She wondered if Rhys had planned it that way. In truth, she was a bit more anxious about moving to a foreign country, even one where English was spoken—more or less. She hoped she would be able to get a job at a bank, for that would make the transition easier.

Ironically, after Lani had agreed to marry Rhys, she rarely saw him alone. All weekend, various members of her family were continually at the cottage. There were so many decisions to be made—about the luau, arranging lodgings for Rhys's partners and his mother and sister, collecting flowers for the leis, and choosing the dances the children would perform at the luau. Since she knew her grandmother wouldn't give her the family wedding dress, she also had to shop for a gown.

It had been Lani's joy to teach her young cousins dances during the last three years. She felt a pang of regret when Bianca volunteered to instruct the children on the steps and gestures of the various dances. Now she would never work with them again, never pass on her knowledge of the Hawaiian culture expressed in dance.

It was only one of the regrets she had about

leaving the island. She knew it was natural and inevitable to have them. Most she kept from Rhys. Especially one.

On Sunday, Emma was released from the hospital. By now, Lani was sure her grandmother knew about her coming marriage. Someone would have told her. It was customary for Tutu to have been asked her permission as a courtesy, and this hadn't been done. That wasn't the only reason Lani wasn't looking forward to seeing her grandmother. It was who she was marrying that would cause the older woman distress.

Lani expected Tutu to be upset, even angry. What she hadn't expected was that her grandmother would refuse to see her.

Choosing a time when Rhys was otherwise occupied, she drove to her grandmother's house. Aku had come for Rhys after lunch to invite him to hunt for the pig for the luau. She was still smiling at the idea of Rhys tramping through the thick tropical jungle where Aku would search for a wild pig. There weren't many undeveloped places left where wild pigs still could be found. Rhys had no idea what he was getting into.

When she arrived, Lani was surprised to find the front door of her grandmother's house locked.

She knocked several times. At last the door was opened, but not by her grandmother. A woman in her fifties stood in the doorway, effectively blocking the entrance.

"Auntie Kay, why is the door locked? Is Tutu here?"

Her aunt looked unusually serious. "She's here."

When Kay didn't move out of the doorway, Lani asked, "Is she all right?"

Kay nodded.

"I'd like to see Tutu," Lani said, puzzled that she had to state the obvious.

Kay shook her head, clearly uncomfortable with the situation. "She won't see you, Lani."

Lani could only stare in shock as her aunt stepped back so she could shut the door. Lani flinched as though she'd been struck when she heard the lock click into place.

She walked stiffly back to her car. For a long time, she simply sat behind the wheel, unable to believe her grandmother had literally shut her out. She no longer had to wonder if Tutu had heard about her decision to marry Rhys. Nor did she have to guess what her reaction was.

Gripping the steering wheel, she lowered her head to rest on her hands. God, what was she doing? she wondered, doubts and fears suddenly assailing her. Was she really going to go to a strange land with a man she'd known for such a short time, away from her family, her friends, and everything she had ever loved? Australia. She didn't know anything about the land down under other than the things she had seen in movies and advertisements.

She swallowed with difficulty as she lifted her head and looked at the house where she had been raised. Memories cascaded over her of leaving that house with her grandmother for her first day of school; of her graduation luau; of Tutu teaching her the *meles*, the dances of Hawaii.

A tear escaped her eye and slowly slid down her cheek. She felt torn, as though she were being ripped in two. Part of her wanted to stay where everything was familiar, where she knew who she was and what she was doing.

Raising her hand, she brushed away the moisture on her cheek and lifted her chin. But if she stayed, she would be without the one person who made her complete. She had a chance for a future with Rhys.

And she was going to take it.

When Lani finally returned to her cottage, she was thankful Rhys wasn't there. She needed time to think about Tutu's attitude and what she was going to do about it. If her grandmother was doing this to force Lani to change her mind, the older woman was going to be disappointed. It wasn't going to work. Lani loved the stubborn, proud lady. She always had and always would. But she needed Rhys. She had made her choice, and it was the right one. It was the only one she could make.

While she waited for Rhys to return, she made another choice. She wasn't going to tell him about the visit to her grandmother's. It wouldn't accomplish anything if he knew Tutu wouldn't see her, much less talk to her.

When Rhys came back, she didn't have to worry about trying to hide her distress over her grandmother. After Aku dropped him off, thankfully taking the results of the day's hunt with him, Rhys searched through the cottage for Lani. Seeing her clothes draped over the foot of the bed, he knew where she was. He changed out of his grungy jeans and shirt, replacing them with a pair of cutoffs before going down to the beach.

Lani was in the water, swimming with strong strokes past the breakwater. He stood on the beach, letting the waves wash over his ankles as he watched her. As badly as he wanted to see her and touch her, he waited patiently. He had all the time in the world. The rest of their lives.

Finally, she rode the crest of a wave in to the shore. And she got to her feet and swept her hair out of her eyes she saw him and smiled. "Hi. Did you have any luck?"

He closed the distance between them and pulled

her into his arms. Her wet body, rather than damp-ening the heat inside him, fanned his desire.

"I can't believe my luck," he murmured huskily. "I'm going to spend the rest of my life with you."

Her eyes glowed with pleasure. Wrapping her arms around his neck, she rose up on her toes. "I was referring to the safari into the wilds of Oahu, but I like your answer."

His fingers combed through the wet strands of her hair and cupped her neck. He brought his head down to cover her mouth with his, passion exploding through him. Sliding his hands down her back, he brought her hips forcefully into the cradle of his thighs.

A wave crashed behind Lani, its powerful surge thrusting her against Rhys. Desire and need were as elemental as the ocean, as hot as the tropical sun.

Rhys felt her tremble against him. Lifting his head, he looked down at her and saw desire shim-mering in the depths of her green eyes. "This is going to be a long week."

Need thickened her voice. "It doesn't have to be."

"Yes, it does." Lifting her up into his arms, he carried her out of the surf. "Your grandmother wouldn't approve of our living together before we're married."

Lani couldn't control her shudder of reaction. She tried to cover it by tightening her arms around his neck, but it didn't work.

He stopped walking. His eyes narrowed as he stared at her and saw the shadows dim her eyes. "What's wrong?"

She didn't meet his gaze. "Nothing's wrong. I'm being carried out of the sea like a scene from *From Here to Eternity*. What could possibly be wrong?"

He released here, holding her waist when she stood in front of him. "I don't know. That's why I asked."

She kissed him. "It's hunger. I'm starving." Taking his arm, she added, "If you aren't going to go for a swim, let's raid the refrigerator."

Walking beside her, Rhys went over what they had been talking about, trying to figure out what had suddenly taken the light out of her eyes. He had mentioned her grandmother as the reason he wasn't spending the nights with her. He didn't like being apart from her for even one night, but he felt he was doing the right thing. Kimo agreed with him. Apparently, Lani didn't.

Several times during the next couple of days, Rhys caught the same expression in her eyes. Even the startling news he had about her father didn't completely eliminate the sad brooding look in her eyes.

They were having a late snack on Wednesday night when he told her about the phone call he had made earlier that day.

"I called Trevor in London to find out what flight they would be on. He told me he had received a phone call from Richard McGregor."

Lani set down the glass of juice she had raised to her mouth. She really didn't want to hear this. "What did he want?"

"Your father asked if you had received the basket. When Trevor told him you had, Richard wanted to know what your reaction had been. Trevor didn't know quite what to say, so he said you had liked it. That answer didn't satisfy your father. He asked what you had thought of what was in the basket."

Lani frowned. "There wasn't anything in the basket."

"That's what Trevor told him."

Rhys pushed back his chair and left the kitchen. A minute later he returned, carrying the basket. He set it on the table.

"When your father said there was something in the basket, he didn't mean the basket was supposed to have contained something. He meant there was something in the basket itself. Your father's instructions are for you to take the basket apart."

Lani glanced at the rustic basket, then up at Rhys. "The man made a basket to give to me so I could take it apart?"

Rhys returned to his chair. "That's about it."

"Are you sure you want to marry me? Obviously, there is insanity on one side of my family."

He smiled at her. "I'll take the chance." He nodded toward the basket. "Crazy people should be humored. Have a go at the basket."

Pushing her plate to one side, she drew the basket over in front of her. "Did your partner give you a hint what I'm supposed to be looking for?"

"Not a one. He just repeated what your father had told him. You're to take the basket apart."

Feeling foolish, Lani began dismantling the woven willow and oak splints. Because the basket hadn't been especially well constructed, it didn't take long. The thick handle had been tightly affixed to the bowl of the basket with thin strips of leather that had to be cut before the handle could be removed. She thought it was odd that so much care and attention had been given to fastening the handle, but then the whole idea of giving her the basket in the first place was strange.

When she was about to place the handle on top of the rest of the basket debris, she noticed something white protruding from one end. Holding it closer, she saw it was a sheet of paper that had been rolled and stuffed into the hollow handle.

She looked at Rhys, who had been watching her take the basket apart. "There's a piece of paper inside."

"See what it says."

It took both of them to ease the coiled paper out of the handle without tearing it to shreds. Once it was free, Lani unrolled it and spread it out on the table.

It was a plain white piece of typing paper with a paragraph of script in the middle of it. At first, she thought it was a letter from her father, until she deciphered the small writing and read aloud: " 'Being of sound mind and body . . .' " Glancing up at Rhys, she said dryly, "That's debatable."

He smiled. "Read what it says."

The handwriting was so tiny, she had difficulty making out some of the words. The gist of the paragraph was that her father, Richard McGregor, was leaving the entire contents of the library in his home to his daughter, Anne McGregor, upon the event of his death. Underneath were several signatures besides his tiny scrawled name.

She handed the paper to Rhys. "You're the lawyer. What am I supposed to do with this?"

He read it and gave it back. "Keep it. It's a codicil to his will, all perfectly legal with witnesses and the date it was written. This paper can be probated along with his will when he dies, and will entitle you to his books, prints, furniture, whatever is in the library of his home."

"Not just books?"

"It states entire contents. Courts tend to take things literally. If your father wanted you to have just the books, he would have worded it differently."

Glancing at it one more time, she shook her head. First he gave her a basket, then the contents of his library. Who knew what that might include, and for a moment she was nonplussed.

But then as she thought about it, a tiny feeling of warmth toward her unknown father crept through her. If he was like most people she knew, he kept his most treasured—if not necessarily valuable—belongings in his library. And he wanted her to have those.

Confused by the unfamiliar feelings whirling through her, she gave the paper back to Rhys and stood up. "Here. Do whatever lawyers do with these things. Richard McGregor is still very much alive, so nothing has to be done about this now."

Rather than argue with her, he folded the paper and slipped it into his pocket. "Your father will want to know you've found it. Either through my partner or from you personally."

She scooped up the remnants of the basket and dropped them into the wastebasket. "I'll write a note and your partner can forward it on to him. Will that do?"

It was going to have to, Rhys thought. At least for now. Once things around them calmed down and they were settled in Australia, perhaps he could convince Lani to communicate further with her father.

When she returned to the table to clear away their dishes, he noticed the haunted sadness was again in her eyes. Each time he had tried to find out what the problem was, she either quickly changed the subject or they were interrupted.

Like now. Bianca didn't bother to knock. She walked in the front door and shouted Lani's name. As Rhys and Lani entered the living room they saw she had brought six children with her, three boys and three girls. Bianca turned on her tape player and said loudly over the music, "I'm having trouble with one of the *meles*."

Taking it for granted Lani would help, Bianca proceeded to line up the children and put them through their paces. Lani glanced at Rhys, smiling at his look of frustration. "She's having trouble with one of the dances."

"I heard," he said dryly.

Lani's smile slipped a little. There had been little opportunity for them to have much time together lately, and it didn't look as if it was going to be any different tonight.

Leaning against a wall, Rhys watched as Lani helped Bianca with the children. At one point she laughed and hugged one of the boys after he had mastered a difficult step. Rhys realized how long it had been since he had heard her laugh or seen her smile so naturally.

Then one of the children said Tutu would like this dance, and Lani's smile disappeared. She turned to the tape player to turn the cassette over, but not before Rhys saw the pain in her eyes.

Ten

Later that evening Rhys rubbed the back of his neck as he paced Kimo's living room. Since he was usually asleep when Kimo came home, he had no idea how long he was going to have to wait, but it didn't matter.

He had cursed himself soundly for several hours after leaving Lani. He had been so busy making plans, so sure he had all the answers, he hadn't realized Lani never mentioned her grandmother or went to visit her. Mr. Sensitivity, he scoffed silently. If he hadn't been so wrapped up in arranging everyone's lives, he might have found the time to notice Lani hadn't gone to see her grandmother.

He ignored the fact that he wasn't supposed to drink coffee and made a pot. His headaches were nonexistent lately, so he thought he could take the chance. As he was pouring the coffee he heard Kimo's car pull into the drive. Taking the cup with him, he walked back into the living room.

When Kimo opened the front door, his brows shot up at the sight of Rhys. His hair was tousled, as though he'd been dragging his hands through it, and his eyes were bloodshot.

Kimo shut the door behind him. "What's this? Is the groom getting the jitters?"

Rhys shook his head. "I know you must be tired, but can you spare a few minutes? There's something I need to talk to you about."

Kimo tossed his satchel on the floor. "Is there any more of that coffee left?"

Rhys went into the kitchen and came back with a steaming cup of coffee. He handed it to the other man, and Kimo sat down on one of his plump armchairs, one leg crossed casually over the other.

It was impossible for Rhys to sit. Continuing his pacing, he got right to the point. "What is your grandmother's reaction to Lani and me getting married?"

"She doesn't like it."

"I have a feeling that's an understatement. Lani hasn't mentioned her at all the last couple of days. It's only just occurred to me that she hasn't been to see her grandmother since Mrs. Makena got home from the hospital. As far as I know, she hasn't even talked to her on the phone. Something's happened between them."

Kimo sipped his coffee. "I don't want to get in the middle of this."

Rhys stopped pacing. "That didn't stop you when I first arrived here. Leaving the island and her family is going to be difficult enough for Lani without having to leave with bad feelings between her and her grandmother. I can't fix anything if I don't know for sure it's broken."

Kimo set his cup down, then got up and walked over to a cabinet. "For this conversation I need something stronger than coffee."

Rhys shook his head when Kimo offered him a

glass of whiskey. "Talk to me, Kimo. I need some answers."

"You aren't going to like them."

"Probably not, but tell me anyway."

Sitting back down in his chair, Kimo took a long swallow of his drink. "Tutu is refusing to see Lani." He continued quickly when he saw the muscles clench in Rhys's jaw. "It will be hard for you to understand my grandmother's thinking. She is giving Lani a taste of what it will be like to be without Tutu. She's hoping to force Lani to see the error of her ways and come back into the Makena fold."

"Lani's cottage has been full of people making the plans for the luau and the wedding. If I'm still considered *kapu*, why isn't the rest of the family staying away?"

"Tutu is very clever. She hasn't forbidden the family to help Lani. She thinks her absence will be enough to show Lani what it will be like without her grandmother's goodwill. We all want Lani to be happy and, apparently, you make her happy. That's good enough for the rest of us."

"She isn't very happy at the moment."

"She knew when she agreed to marry you how her grandmother would feel. She's made her choice."

"Is there any chance Mrs. Makena will change her mind? Lani will be deeply hurt if her grandmother doesn't come to the wedding."

Kimo finished his drink. "I wouldn't count on it. Tutu can be one stubborn lady."

Rhys slumped down onto the couch. "So there's nothing I can do, nothing I can say to Mrs. Makena to change her mind?"

"I don't know what it would be. You're taking her little girl away, just like another Englishman tried to do with Lahela. Tutu won that battle, probably the same way she's trying to win this one."

Leaning forward, Rhys rested his arms on his thighs. "Are you telling me the reason Lani's mother didn't go with Richard McGregor is because Mrs. Makena stopped her?"

"Oh, she didn't force her. My mother was talking about the past the other night. This situation with Lani reminded her of the treatment Lahela got from Tutu all those years ago. My mother is only a year older than Lani's. She remembers how Tutu wore Lahela down, and how upset Lahela was when Richard McGregor left the island. My mother is on Lani's side this time. I think most of the rest of the family is, too."

Rhys sat back. Kimo had given him a lot to think about, but not much to go on to change Emma Makena's mind. There might not be anything he could do.

But for Lani's sake, he had to try.

Lani didn't think things could get more hectic. The next couple of days showed her she was wrong. On Thursday Rhys met the flights bringing one of his partners from England and his mother and sister from Australia. Only Trevor Pritchard had been able to come, their other partner unable to get away due to business commitments. They were all taken to their respective rooms in the Outrigger Hotel.

Rhys met Lani at the bank at the end of the day and took her to the hotel. His partner had crashed in his room after the long flight, but a brief rest that afternoon had been enough for Rhys's mother and sister. They were seated at an outdoor table where they could enjoy the sights and sounds of the beach. Rhys introduced his mother first, a cheerful woman who was pleased with the plumeria lei Lani placed around her neck. Beryl Berkeley-Jones gave the appearance of being fragile, yet strong, and her accent was slightly broader than Rhys's. Her frank gaze examined Lani thoroughly, and she apparently approved of the woman who was to marry her son.

His sister, Valerie, was introduced next. Her smile was a little more reserved than her mother's, although she also hugged Lani after receiving a lei. She was younger than Rhys by three years, her hair a lighter blond and cut in a casual short style. She also had the same dry sense of humor as her brother.

Both women began to talk almost simultaneously about the flight from Australia, the food on the plane, the drive from the airport, the upcoming wedding, and Rhys's tan. Rhys sat back in his chair, a smile curving his lips as his mother and sister talked in tandem.

Lani sorted out the questions from the comments and answered as many as she could. The topic uppermost in their minds was the reason they had come to the island—the wedding. They wanted to know all the details; where it was going to be, how many people were expected to attend, and especially what they should wear.

Earlier, Rhys had assured her his mother and sister would approve of the wedding plans, but Lani watched their faces carefully as she described the place where the wedding was to be held.

"It is tradition in my family to be married in the ginger garden at Waimea Falls on the north shore of the island. It's a beautiful area where a number of my ancestors lived at one time. It's fairly informal." She smiled at Rhys. "Rhys didn't seem too disappointed he didn't have to wear a tuxedo."

"It sounds lovely," Beryl said. "I know you must

be incredibly busy since everything is so rushed. If there is anything we can do to help, you have only to ask."

"As far as I know," Lani said, "we have everything under control. Rhys and my cousin Kimo have been doing most of the work."

"When can we meet your family?" Beryl asked. "Rhys has told us you were raised by your grandmother. She sounds like a lovely woman. I'm looking forward to meeting her."

Only Rhys noticed the way Lani's smile wavered for a moment. "My grandmother was in a minor car accident recently and is recovering from several injuries. We aren't sure she will be able to attend the wedding."

Beryl looked disappointed but accepted the news graciously. Rhys changed the subject, asking his mother if she would like to have dinner and see a Polynesian show featuring members of Lani's family. Both women didn't hesitate. They would love to see a show and meet some of Lani's family. But first, could they do a little shopping?

Rhys laughed. To Lani he said, "I'm surprised they waited this long before demanding to see the shops. I expected to be ordered to stop at the first shopping mall we passed on the way to the hotel."

What followed was a good-natured teasing bout between Rhys and his family. Lani enjoyed seeing this different side of the man she was going to marry. He was relaxed and comfortable, giving as good as he got during the spirited exchange.

The rest of the evening followed a similar pattern of cheerful conversation mixed with affection and humor. Rhys's mother responded with infectious joy to everything she did and saw. Even the simplest thing—the colorful pattern of a dress, the delicate petals of a hibiscus, or the small vanda orchid floating on top of the Mai Tai she had ordered at Trader Vic's.

Immediately after Kimo's performance, Beryl suggested they return to their room at the hotel. The long plane trip and all the exciting things she had seen had worn her out. She would be fine in the morning after a good rest, and be ready to go to a few shops and see some of the marvelous sights on the island.

During the drive to her cottage after seeing Valerie and Beryl to their rooms, Lani was still chuckling over some of the amusing comments Rhys's mother had made.

"Your mother has a wonderful way of looking at the world. Has she always been like that?"

"As long as I can remember." He glanced at her, smiling broadly. "The day of the wedding, I've arranged for Aku to bring my mother and sister to Waimea Falls. It should be an interesting trip, don't you think?"

Lani burst out laughing. "It would be worth the price of admission."

Rhys drove into Lani's driveway and parked the car. He was no longer smiling. "I know my mother. Tomorrow she will ask me to take her to see your grandmother. She will bring her flowers and get-well wishes. She'll say how pleased she is her son is marrying such a beautiful woman, inside and out. Then she'll tell your grandmother she hopes she will be able to attend the wedding."

Lani gave him a look of horror. "She can't do that."

"I can guarantee it's what she'll want to do. My mother will want to meet her because she's your grandmother and because she's been injured. Those two reasons are good enough for her to insist on a visit to your grandmother's house."

"Your mother isn't going to understand when she's not allowed even to see my grandmother."

Rhys shifted to face her. "Is that what happened when you went to see her?"

She wondered how he knew. Forcing away her pain, she said, "If she won't see me, it's doubtful she will see your mother. I wouldn't want your mother to be hurt, Rhys. You'll have to find some way to convince her not to try to see Tutu."

Rhys was silent for a moment. Maybe Emma Makena and Beryl Berkeley-Jones should meet, he mused. It would be even more interesting than a meeting between his mother and Aku.

He reached for her hand. "Is the price becoming too high to pay, Lani?"

She looked puzzled. "Price for what?"

"The price of being with me."

Her fingers tightened in his, and she brought his hand up between her breasts. "Whatever the price is, I'll pay it."

He had to struggle to keep from pulling her into his arms. If he did, he wouldn't be able to stop at just a few kisses. Looking into her eyes, he saw the warmth of desire beginning to flare in them. They were eyes a man could drown in. He had, and he didn't want to be rescued.

Leaning over, he touched her lips with his. When he started to lift his head, she moved toward him, maintaining the contact. She spread his fingers out on her breast, sighing when he couldn't resist stroking the soft flesh.

"Lani, I promised," he murmured against her mouth.

"I know. You promised Kimo you wouldn't sleep with me until the wedding."

He heard the strain in her voice. It matched the tension within him. Taking a deep breath, he removed his hand and sat back. "When I promised Kimo to leave you alone until the wedding, I thought it might show your grandmother I'm not just using you. Now I know it wouldn't make any difference to your grandmother. But I gave my word."

"I understand. I don't like it, but I do understand."

"It will only be two more days. Then we'll be together for the rest of our lives."

Two days sounded like forever. "Will you drive me to work in the morning? You'll need my car again to take your mother and sister shopping. I can call Bianca and ride in with her if it's easier."

"I'll take you. We hardly see each other as it is and the next couple of days aren't going to be much different."

Lani hesitated before reaching for the latch. Her breast still ached from his brief touch, and the kiss had been too fleeting. Each night it was more and more difficult to say good night and spend the rest of the evening apart.

When she started to open the door, he stopped her. "Wait. I have something for you."

Turning back, she looked at him. "You didn't have to get me anything, Rhys."

"It's something you should have had days ago. I had to wait for it to be made."

He took a small box out of his pocket and opened the hinged top. Inside was a ring, designed so that a flat miniature wave was curving around a flawless diamond.

"Rhys," she breathed. "It's the most beautiful ring I've ever seen."

He slipped it on her finger. "I thought it would be like taking a piece of the island with you when you leave."

"I love it." She flung her arms around his neck. "I love you."

He held her tightly, his lips skimming over her

throat. "I love you." Unable to resist, he kissed her deeply. Frustrated passion twisted through him as he sought the intimate warmth of her mouth. He had to fight the urge to draw her down onto the seat.

His hands shook as he pulled her wrists from around his neck. "Saturday better get here quickly."

She slumped against him for a moment, then straightened. "I should be glad you're a man who keeps his word, but right now I wish you would say to hell with your promise and come into the cottage with me."

"There's nothing I want more." Holding her away from him, he gazed seriously at her. "If your grandmother learns I'm staying in your cottage, it might ruin the chance of convincing her to come to the wedding."

Lani sighed. "Rhys, forget it. Tutu won't change her mind. I've accepted it, you have to. There's nothing that can be done about her attitude."

"I can't accept that. I don't understand how you can give up so easily."

She sat back, leaning against the door. "It hasn't been easy."

He heard the hurt and sadness in her voice. "I'm sorry. Of course it hasn't been easy. It's just that I still think there is something we can do. I want our wedding day to be the happiest day of your life. Your grandmother is an important part of your life. She should be there."

He didn't understand, Lani thought. Nothing would make Tutu change her mind.

The day of the wedding dawned bright and sunny. Bianca used her key to let herself into Lani's cottage earlier than she was expected. When she heard the shower running, she yelled to let Lani know she was there.

Lani turned off the water. Opening the sliding-glass door, she grabbed a towel and called, "What are you doing here so early?"

"I brought you something."

Lani wrapped the towel around herself, tucking it in between her breasts, and stepped into her bedroom. Bianca was already dressed for the wedding in a slim-fitting royal blue dress, a pink hibiscus worn above one ear. She was standing in front of the bed as though guarding it.

She was also grinning and looking very pleased with herself.

Lani put her hands on her hips. "What's wrong with you?"

"Remember last night when we were stringing leis and my mother said it was a shame you wouldn't be able to wear the Makena wedding dress?"

"Of course I remember. I don't like talking about it any better now than I did last night."

"Well, we don't need to talk about it ever again." She stood to one side and swept her arm toward the bed.

Behind her was a plastic-wrapped dress on a padded satin hanger. Lani slowly walked over to the bed. Lifting the plastic carefully from the dress, she uncovered a white gown with a high neck, ruffles across the bodice, and narrow sleeves that were puffed at the top. The dress was old-fashioned, but Lani loved its traditional style. It was the Makena wedding dress.

"I don't know what to say," she murmured, her voice thick with emotion.

"Say you'll wear it."

She slipped it off the hanger and held it in front of her as she stood before the mirror. "Of course I'll wear it. I hope it fits. There isn't much time to make alterations." She turned from one side to the other, her arm clasped around the waist of the dress as she gazed at herself. "How did you get Tutu to agree to let me have it?"

"Well . . ." Bianca suddenly found a piece of lint on the front of her dress that required her attention.

Lani lowered the gown. Turning to look at her cousin, she asked, "How did you get it then?"

"Mama helped. She kept Tutu occupied while I took it out of the trunk." Seeing Lani's grim expression, she added, "I'll take it back after the wedding. You have a right to wear it, Lani. It's not your fault Tutu is being so darned stubborn."

Lani sank down onto her bed, still holding the dress. "I was hoping Tutu had given in."

Bianca sat beside her. "That is one stubborn lady. Maybe that's where you get it from."

"I want to marry the man I love. That isn't being stubborn."

"How is the prospective groom holding up?"

"I haven't seen him since he drove me to work yesterday morning. He called me at the bank and said his mother had this superstition about the groom not seeing the bride before the wedding. That's why I called you to get a ride home last night."

Bianca stood up. "As bridesmaid, I'm supposed to help you get ready, so let's get to it."

The sun had burned the dew off the grass hours before Lani arrived at Waimea Falls with Bianca. The scent of plumeria blossoms filled the air, and the sound of thrushes singing in the trees added to the exotic outdoor setting. Much of her family had already gathered on the expanse of grass covering the area known as the ginger garden.

Many of the children had gone to the falls while

the adults spread rattan mats and blankets on the grass and talked excitedly about the wedding. Lani watched as Luka tugged at his older brother's hand to hurry him along to the falls, and she remembered all the times she had done the same thing to Kimo. Even though they were the same age, she hadn't been allowed to go to the falls unless Kimo was with her.

It would be impossible to count the times she had come to Waimea Falls with her family. It would be impossible not to think of all the celebrations she would miss in the future. A strange ache was centered in her chest. She hadn't even left the island, and she was already homesick.

Her smile was shaky as Pami slipped a pikake-flower lei over her head and kissed her, wishing her *aloha nui loa*, much love. Other leis followed with hugs and kisses from various members of her family. She was surrounded by the love and closeness she had always known—and would miss.

She had turned to accept best wishes from another aunt when she saw Rhys walking toward the garden. Her sadness vanished instantly. He was dressed in white with a red satin sash around his waist and a trailing lei of green maile leaves draped over his shoulders. She hadn't expected him to wear the traditional Hawaiian wedding apparel. The man walking beside him was also dressed in white, although without the sash.

Rhys felt his heart skip when he saw Lani standing among her family. A wreath of leaves and flowers crowned her head, her shining hair flowing over her shoulders. The skirt of the long white dress flowed around her ankles as she walked toward him.

Stopping in front of him, she smiled. "Hi."

He needed to touch her. Threading his fingers

through hers, he held on to her hand tightly.
"Hi."

For a moment they simply looked at each other,
their gazes saying how glad they were to see each
other. The sound of someone clearing his throat
brought them back to the present. Smiling, Rhys
introduced his partner and best man.

Trevor Pritchard was as tall as Rhys, his gray
eyes shielded by horn-rim glasses. He murmured
he was pleased to meet her as she shook his
hand.

"I'm pleased to meet you, Mr. Pritchard. I believe I have you to thank for a basket that is no
longer a basket."

The smile he gave her was a slightly self-conscious.
"I admit it was an odd request, Miss McGregor."

"Please call me Lani." Glancing around, she
asked, "Where's your mother and Valerie?"

"They'll be here. Aku is bringing them from the
hotel."

"And what about Kimo? I thought he would be
coming with you."

Rhys smiled at her slightly irritated tone. "He
had something to do. He'll be here later."

Lani couldn't imagine what Kimo had to do
that was more important than her wedding. Rhys
didn't give her time to dwell on his absence,
though. Bringing her with him, he proceeded to
introduce Trevor to Bianca and several other members of Lani's family. Leis were given to him, along
with kisses on his cheek. At first, he appeared
startled by the attention and the casual accep-
tance. By the time Bianca slipped her arm through
his, he was so bemused, he simply patted her hand
and left it there.

With Trevor in good hands, Rhys drew Lani
away from the crowd. He reached out and fin-
gered a delicate pikake blossom in one of the leis.

"There's still time to change your mind, Lani. I've rushed you into this without giving you many choices. I'm giving you a choice now. I want you to marry me and go to Australia because I love you and can't imagine living the rest of my life without you. It's up to you."

She smiled up at him, all of her love shining in her eyes. "One of the things you're going to learn about me over the next fifty or so years is that I rarely do anything I don't want to do. My grandmother didn't understand that and she's known me all my life. She tried to force me to stay here, but I don't want to stay if you aren't going to be here."

He drew her into his arms and held her, simply held her against him. He had his answer. His arms tightened. Thank God, he had his answer.

Behind them, they heard the crowd suddenly call out, shouting and laughing. A group began to sing a Hawaiian song of joy and welcome. Keeping his arm around her waist, Rhys moved aside so Lani could see what all the excitement was about.

A woman on crutches was slowly making her way toward the ginger garden. On one side of her was Kimo, on the other was Aku. Behind them were Beryl and Valerie, gaily dressed in bright flowery muumuus.

Lani blinked rapidly against the tears that sprang to her eyes. "What made Tutu change her mind?" she asked in a low voice, thick with emotion.

"My mother had a wee chat with her."

She swiped away a few tears. "I don't know what she could possibly have said, but I'm glad she did."

"She gave her word that you and I would return to the island once a year. The rest I don't know. I wasn't there and my mother told me I didn't need to know." Tightening his arm around her, he bent down and kissed her. "Now we can get married."

The sun shone brightly on them as they walked toward the meadow where the ceremony was to be held. When Lani approached her grandmother, she removed one of the pikake leis and slipped it over the older woman's head.

"*Aloha nui loa*, Tutu."

Emma shifted her gaze from Lani to the tall man standing beside her granddaughter. Leaning on her crutches, she gestured for Rhys to come closer. When he stepped in front of her, she motioned for him to bend down. She lifted the lei over his head, saying softly, "No *kapu*."

Rhys kissed her cheek, then his mother's before taking Lani's arm to walk over to the minister dressed in a long flowing white robe.

With their family around them, they exchanged vows spoken first in Hawaiian, then in English. Under the canopy of a kukui nut tree, they exchanged rings. Their life together had begun.

THE EDITOR'S CORNER

1990. A new decade. I suspect that most of us who are involved in romance publishing will remember the 1980s as "the romance decade." During the past ten years we have seen a momentous change as Americans jumped into the romance business and developed the talent and expertise to publish short, contemporary American love stories. Previously the only romances of this type had come from British and Australian authors through the Canadian company, Harlequin Enterprises. That lonely giant, or monopoly, was first challenged in the early 1980s when Dell published Ecstasy romances under Vivien Stephens's direction; by Simon and Schuster, which established Silhouette romances (now owned by Harlequin); and by Berkley/Jove, which supported my brainchild, Second Chance at Love. After getting that line off to a fine start, I came to Bantam.

The times had grown turbulent by the middle of the decade. But an industry had been born. Editors who liked and understood romance had been found and trained. Enormous numbers of writers had been discovered and were flocking to workshops and seminars sponsored by the brand-new Romance Writers of America to acquire or polish their skills.

LOVESWEPT was launched with six romances in May 1983. And I am extremely proud of all the wonderful authors who've been with us through these seven years and who have never left the fold, no matter the inducements to do so. I'm just as proud of the LOVESWEPT staff. There's been very little turnover—Susann Brailey, Nita Taublib, and Elizabeth Barrett have been on board all along; Carrie Feron and Tom Kleh have been here a year and two years, respectively. I'm also delighted by you, our readers, who have so wholeheartedly endorsed every innovation we've dared to make—our authors publishing under their real names and including pictures and autobiographies in their books, and the Fan of the Month feature, which puts the spotlight on a person who represents many of our readers. And of course I thank you for all your kind words about the Editor's Corner.

Now, starting this new decade, we find there wasn't enough growth in the audience for romances and/or there was too much being published, so that most American publishers have left the arena. It is only big Harlequin and little LOVESWEPT. Despite our small size, we are as vigorous and hearty, excited and exuberant now as we were in the beginning. I can't wait to see what the next ten years bring. What LOVESWEPT innova-

(continued)

tions do you imagine I might be summarizing in the Editor's Corner as we head into the new *century*?

But now to turn from musings about the year 2000 to the very real pleasures of next month!

Let Iris Johansen take you on one of her most thrilling, exciting journeys to Sedikhan, read **NOTORIOUS,** LOVESWEPT #378. It didn't matter to Sabin Wyatt that the jury had acquitted gorgeous actress Mallory Thane of his stepbrother's murder. She had become his obsession. He cleverly gets her to Sedikhan and confronts her with a demand that she tell him the truth about her marriage. When she does, he refuses to believe her story. He will believe only what he can feel: primitive, consuming desire for Mallory. . . . Convinced that Mallory returns his passion, Sabin takes her in fiery and unforgettable moments. That's only the beginning of **NOTORIOUS,** which undoubtedly is going onto my list of all-time favorites from Iris. I bet you, too, will label this romance a keeper.

Here comes another of Gail Douglas's fabulous romances about the sisters, *The Dreamweavers,* whose stories never fail to enmesh me and hold me spellbound. In LOVESWEPT #379, **SOPHISTICATED LADY,** we meet the incredible jazz pianist Pete Cochrane. When he looks up from the keyboard into Lisa Sinclair's eyes, he is captivated by the exquisite honey-blonde. He begins to play Ellington's "Sophisticated Lady," and Ann is stunned by the potent appeal of this musical James Bond. These two vagabonds have a rocky road to love that we think you'll relish every step of the way.

What a delight to welcome back Jan Hudson with her LOVESWEPT #380, **ALWAYS FRIDAY.** Full of fun and laced with fire, **ALWAYS FRIDAY** introduces us to handsome executive Daniel Friday and darling Tess Cameron. From the very first, Tess knows that there's no one better to unstarch Dan's collars and teach him to cut loose from his workaholism. Dan fears he can't protect his free-spirited and sexy Tess from disappointment. It's a glorious set of problems these two confront and solve.

Next, in Peggy Webb's **VALLEY OF FIRE,** LOVESWEPT #381, you are going to meet a dangerous man. A very dangerous and exciting man. I'd be surprised if you didn't find Rick McGill, the best private investigator in Tupelo, Mississippi, the stuff that the larger-than-life Sam Spades are made of with a little Valentino thrown in. Martha Ann Riley summons all her courage to dare to play Bacall to Rick's Bogart. She wants to find her sister's gambler husband . . . and turns out to be Rick's

(continued)

perfect companion for a sizzling night in a cave, a wicked romp through Las Vegas. Wildly attracted, Martha Ann thinks Rick is the most irresistible scoundrel she's ever met . . . and the most untrustworthy! Don't miss **VALLEY OF FIRE!** It's fantastic.

Glenna McReynolds gives us her most ambitious and thrilling romance to date in LOVESWEPT #382, **DATELINE: KYDD AND RIOS.** Nobody knew more about getting into trouble than Nikki Kydd, but that talent had made her perfect at finding stories for Josh Rios, the daring photojournalist who'd built his career reporting the battles and betrayals of San Simeon's dictatorship. After three years as partners, when he could resist her no longer, he ordered Nikki back to the States—but in the warm, dark tropical night he couldn't let her go . . . without teaching the green-eyed witch her power as a woman. She'd vanished with the dawn rather than obey Josh's command to leave, but now, a year later, Nikki needs him back . . . to fulfill a desperate bargain.

What a treat you can expect from Fayrene Preston next month—the launch book of her marvelous quartet about the people who live and work in a fabulous house, SwanSea Place. Here in LOVESWEPT #383, *SwanSea Place:* **THE LEGACY,** Caitlin Deverell had been born in SwanSea, the magnificent family home on the wild, windswept coast of Maine, and now she was restoring its splendor to open it as a luxury resort. When Nico DiFrenza asked her to let him stay for a few days, caution demanded she refuse the mysterious visitor's request—but his spellbinding charm made that impossible! So begins a riveting tale full of the unique charm Fayrene can so wonderfully invent for us.

Altogether a spectacular start to the new decade with great LOVESWEPT reading.

Warm good wishes,

Carolyn Nichols

Carolyn Nichols
Editor
LOVESWEPT
Bantam Books
666 Fifth Avenue
New York, NY 10103

FAN OF THE MONTH

Hazel Parker

Twelve years ago my husband Hoke insisted that I quit my job as a data processor to open a paperback bookstore. The reason was that our book bill had become as large as our grocery bill. Today I am still in the book business, in a much larger store, still reading and selling my favorite romance novels.

My most popular authors are of course writing for what I consider to be the number one romance series— LOVESWEPT. One of the all-time favorites is Kay Hooper. Her books appeal to readers because of her sense of humor and unique characters (for instance, Pepper in **PEPPER'S WAY**). And few authors can write better books than Iris Johansen's **THE TRUST-WORTHY REDHEAD** or Fayrene Preston's **FOR THE LOVE OF SAMI.** When the three authors get together (as they did for the Delaney series), you have *dynamite*. Keep up the good work, LOVESWEPT.

60 Minutes to a Better, More Beautiful You!

Now it's easier than ever to awaken your sensuality, stay slim forever—even make yourself irresistible. With Bantam's bestselling subliminal audio tapes, you're only 60 minutes away from a better, more beautiful you!

__	45004-2	**Slim Forever**	$8.95
__	45112-X	**Awaken Your Sensuality**	$7.95
__	45081-6	**You're Irresistible**	$7.95
__	45035-2	**Stop Smoking Forever**	$8.95
__	45130-8	**Develop Your Intuition**	$7.95
__	45022-0	**Positively Change Your Life**	$8.95
__	45154-5	**Get What You Want**	$7.95
__	45041-7	**Stress Free Forever**	$7.95
__	45106-5	**Get a Good Night's Sleep**	$7.95
__	45094-8	**Improve Your Concentration**	$7.95
__	45172-3	**Develop A Perfect Memory**	$8.95

THE DELANEY DYNASTY

Men and women whose loves an passions are so glorious
it takes many great romance novels by three bestselling
authors to tell their tempestuous stories.

THE SHAMROCK TRINITY

☐	21975	RAFE, THE MAVERICK *by Kay Hooper*	$2.95
☐	21976	YORK, THE RENEGADE *by Iris Johansen*	$2.95
☐	21977	BURKE, THE KINGPIN *by Fayrene Preston*	$2.95

THE DELANEYS OF KILLAROO

☐	21872	ADELAIDE, THE ENCHANTRESS *by Kay Hooper*	$2.75
☐	21873	MATILDA, THE ADVENTURESS *by Iris Johansen*	$2.75
☐	21874	SYDNEY, THE TEMPTRESS *by Fayrene Preston*	$2.75

THE DELANEYS: *The Untamed Years*

☐	21899	GOLDEN FLAMES *by Kay Hooper*	$3.50
☐	21898	WILD SILVER *by Iris Johansen*	$3.50
☐	21897	COPPER FIRE *by Fayrene Preston*	$3.50

Buy them at your local bookstore or use this page to order.

· Bantam Books, Dept. SW7, 414 East Golf Road, Des Plaines, IL 60016

Please send me the items I have checked above. I am enclosing $_____
(please add $2.00 to cover postage and handling). Send check or money
order, no cash or C.O.D.s please.

Mr/Ms _____

Address _____

City/State _____ Zip _____

SW7–11/89

Please allow four to six weeks for delivery.
Prices and availability subject to change without notice.

THE LATEST IN BOOKS
AND AUDIO CASSETTES